Broken Bodyguard

The Nightingales of Wall Street #1
Ember Leigh

Published by Ember Leigh, 2024

EmberLeighAuthor@gmail.com

Cover art: Covers by Combs

Editing: Brandi Zelenka

Contents

ABOUT THE BOOK

The hulking teddy bear I met at a Christmas party last month is a bodyguard – a scorching hot single one – but I know better than to think he'd be interested in a curvy single mom like me.

It doesn't matter that I can't stop thinking about him. My only priority now is getting my life back on track after my ex. Even though said ex is determined to make things miserable for me...and when he crosses a line, suddenly *I* need a bodyguard.

Luckily, I know a guy. And he's more than willing to whisk me away to safety. The only problem is, the longer we spend in this remote Kentucky cabin, the harder it is to imagine what life looks like after *this*.

I'm positive I can keep my head on straight...until Troy shows me all the ways he's interested in me. All the parts of me that I see as broken, he sees as beautiful.

Something between us has me throwing logic out the window.

He's a free-floating bachelor, and about to leave the country for a new assignment. I'm a 1st grade teacher with a three-year-old. In what universe does this make sense?

While it seems there's no way forward for us, my heart is ready to do whatever it takes to make this fantasy become a reality.

Even though my ex is dead-set on the opposite.

CHAPTER ONE

TROY

"Any chance you're heading south soon?"

The soft urgency in Mercedes's question broke through the din of the Manhattan restaurant. All around us, conversation roared inside the upscale Italian eatery. Our plates were empty in front of us, awaiting the renowned lasagnas and cacio e pepe that the Fairchild party had ordered. Dining out with this crew was always a lavish affair, and I had no problem enjoying the spoils.

I looked over at her, trying to figure out what 'south' she referred to. I must have taken too long to answer because she hurried to add, "Southern US." She offered a small smile, but there was worry tugging at the corners of her eyes.

"I might be," I told her, reaching for my frosted glass of beer. They never gave you the bottles in places like this, so I was forced to look like a cultured man. "What's going on?"

Mercedes glanced at Willow, who sat between her and Trace at the long table, drawing on a pad of paper they'd brought along. Then she drew a deep breath, leaning closer to me. "If you were heading in that direction, I was thinking of asking you for a favor."

I took a pull of beer. I was always heading in a new direction. I'd ended a six-month stint in Los Angeles back in November, and then I'd come to New York for a holiday breather, though I'd accidentally picked up a couple gigs while I was visiting. My life was like that.

Always fun, always a surprise, always on the go. And I had no intention of stopping or settling down.

I didn't know anything but transience. Since day one.

"It sounds like you need me to head in that direction." I lifted a brow.

"I just thought that, well—" She expelled a worried burst of air, her hands finding the bump of her belly. She'd revealed a month ago that she and Trace were expecting, and it was cool to see her growing in real time. "Do you remember my sister-in-law Maddie?"

I was mid-sip when she asked the question, and the beer went down the wrong pipe. I coughed, damn near choking.

Remember Maddie? That brunette with all the curves, the soft smile, and the most infectious laughter I'd heard since...I didn't even fucking know when? The sugar sweet schoolteacher with the little girl on her hip who'd made Jordan and Seven's Christmas party evaporate in the blink of an eye as we chatted in the far corner?

Yeah, I fucking remembered her.

Couldn't stop thinking about her, either.

"Yeah," I said, setting my beer back on the table. A safe, non-choking distance away. "Is she coming north again, or...?" My heart rate picked up. Thankfully, Mercedes wouldn't catch on to that. I didn't make a habit of lusting after single moms who lived a thousand miles away from my security gig du jour. With my lifestyle I knew better than that.

Still, Maddie had burrowed into my brain. And even a month after our goodbyes, I still thought about her every day. I'd stopped myself from begging for Maddie's number more times than I cared to admit.

Mercedes was just about to respond when a wave of raucous greetings overcame our conversation. Trace surged to his feet at Mercedes's side, followed by his brothers Axel and Damian farther down the table. I couldn't see yet who had arrived, but those three brothers knew just about everyone in Manhattan, either from advising them on their finances and investments or from rubbing elbows with them in elite circles. My best friend Seven, sitting across the table with his girlfriend Jordan, also seemed to recognize the newcomer because he pushed to standing and came around the table. I didn't really care who was here. I needed to know what Mercedes had to say about Maddie.

"I can't believe you had a reservation for the same time." Trace's voice boomed as he pulled the newcomer into a quick bro hug. I caught a flash of tattoos creeping down a manly forearm. I cleared my throat, ready to prompt Mercedes again, when Trace shouted my name.

"Trojan! I need you for a second." Trace waved me to standing, his dark eyes shining with mischief. "I've been talking you up to this guy for too long."

Now my gig radar was pinging. I had the distant urge to tell Trace to wait until my conversation with Mercedes was over, but even Mercedes looked excited by whoever was here.

I pushed my chair back from the table. Trace, Axel, and Damian owned Fairchild Enterprises on Wall Street, a successful and well-known wealth management company. After their company had been investigated by the SEC for financial fraud, the ensuing drama and ultimate name-clearing could be made into a high-drama Netflix series. If the investigation had hindered their business in any way, it certainly didn't show. The brothers were more famous than some of the A-list actors we occasionally saw out on the town.

The Fairchilds had gathered around the newcomer at the end of the table. I joined them, nodding at the brawny, suited man. He almost passed for any other Wall Street type—button-up shirt, sleeves rolled back, pressed black pants—except for the tattoos. His arms were covered in ink, and some crept past the collar of his shirt as well.

"Nash. I've been wanting you to meet this one. He's the CPO I've been talking about." Trace's dark eyes gleamed as he clapped my back, which only made me stand taller. At six four, I was the tallest one here—but Trace and this Nash guy were close seconds. "Trojan, meet Nash Nightingale."

Nash stuck out a hand, which I shook firmly. His eyes were a dizzying shade of blue, something between clouds and lake ice.

"Trojan, it's great to finally meet you. You come highly recommended."

I looked around at the Fairchild brothers. "I didn't realize I was being recommended."

"We are perpetually recommending you," Axel said with a grin. To Nash, he said, "If you need a connection, this guy has got it. He pulled an ex-CIA operative out of his ass for us once when we needed one."

Nash smiled in a calculating way. His gaze hadn't moved from me, and I could tell he was sizing me up for something. Though I didn't know what for, I was more intrigued than I wanted to let on. The Fairchilds were part of my inner circle now, so I trusted their judgement. Which was why whatever Mercedes was about to ask me to do, I already knew my answer. And if the brothers were talking me up to a potential employer, I could bank on it being a good next gig.

"I've got more where he came from." I cracked a grin, and Axel burst into laughter.

"Trojan is best friends with Seven, who heads our family's security detail," Trace told Nash. "They're old military buddies turned security experts."

"Why haven't you joined your friend's business?" Nash asked quickly. The question almost caused me to take a step back. I could sense the awareness behind the question. Astute, this one.

"Seven has his own firm," I explained, "which is New York-focused. I, on the other hand, want to keep traveling the world while skirting complicated tax returns."

Nash grinned, nodding. "So traveling is important to you?"

"Among other things."

"Very diplomatic way of saying he's going to need a very high salary," Axel added. I was ready to elbow Axel—not because he was wrong, but because it thrust us into salary talks when our appetizers were just about to arrive *and* I could barely pry my mind off what I might learn about Maddie at the other end of the table. But this was how business deals worked in Manhattan. It was breakneck or nothing.

"A high salary will be no problem," Nash said smoothly. His white-toothed grin and understated but expensive-as-hell rings struck me as right on par for the elite circles I'd heard about through Seven. But Nash also had a rough edge that I couldn't quite put my finger on. Like he wasn't from here, or if he was, he hadn't come from wealth.

"As long as the work ethic is there and long hours aren't an issue," Nash went on. "I'll be honest, I don't want to hire anyone that doesn't come with a recommendation like you've gotten from the Fairchilds. Close protection officers are a dime a dozen, but the good ones are harder to find. And I haven't come across a single CPO with a recommendation like yours."

Nash's words hung in the air, and for a moment, the entire restaurant shrank away. Somehow, I was on the cusp of a job offer. Ten minutes ago, I'd been debating between red or cream sauce. The time was right, though. I was nearing the end of my current short-term gig here in the city, which meant I needed to figure out where I was heading next. This was the life of a qualified CPO who didn't like to stay in one place for too long.

"What sort of protection are you looking for?" I noticed Trace, Damian, and Axel had quietly faded away, leaving Nash and me to negotiate on our own. I stuffed my hands into the pockets of my khakis. If I had to negotiate a new contract while waiting for lasagna, so be it. *Wall Street, I'll play the game your way.*

Nash took a step closer, his ice-blue gaze darting around as though searching for spies. When he spoke, his voice had dropped a few decibels. "My brother and I have experienced a...change in income. We're eager to hire someone who can come along for the ride and be okay with a slightly more unconventional approach than what's typical in Manhattan. We're not looking for protection from the paparazzi. We need protection from...haters. The occasional kidnapper. Things like that."

Something clicked inside with the use of the word 'hater'. The Fairchilds were the kings of unconventional on Wall Street and had garnered their own set of enemies. From the sound of it, Nash Nightingale was new money, much like the Fairchilds had been when they came onto the scene a decade ago. It only made sense they'd befriend someone like this. And as for the occasional kidnapper...that was par for the course with most wealthy people. They were usually targets for thieves, whether for robbery, or a well-timed hostage situation that led to a hefty ransom.

Nash needed an outsider. Like he was. Like the Fairchilds were. Like I was.

"Trust me, I have no allegiance to how things are done in Manhattan," I told him. "My last gig was in California, and before that, Paris. I've worked in ten countries over the last five years. Consider me a neutral party."

Nash's dental ad grin grew even wider. "Good. I'm a little tired of the rules here, and I'd like to find somebody that has a broader perspective."

"Broad and willing," I cracked.

"How do you feel about a trial run?" Nash's dark brow lifted imperceptibly. "A few weeks in Ecuador. We're leaving next week. You come with us, get to know me and my brother, and then we can see how we feel about terms moving forward."

Ecuador. A few weeks. Equal likelihood of this turning out to be a drug deal or investment opportunity, but either way, I was down for the adventure. "Sounds like a plan." I fished out a business card from my wallet, handing it to Nash. "Send me the travel info, where we should meet, all the details. Plus your salary offer. I'll be there."

Nash pocketed the card, offering me a final handshake just as the server appeared with a steaming tray of food. "Enjoy your meal, Trojan. It was great to meet you."

Nash strode further into the restaurant, and I returned to my seat to a round of cheers from the brothers.

"Done deal or what?" Damian asked as he slung his arm around his girlfriend Jessa.

"We're going to South America together." I laid my napkin back in my lap, watching as the server set out small platters of oysters, scallops, and crabcakes. "Feels pretty done to me."

"Sounds like you guys are already end game," Axel said.

"Things happen fast in the Fairchild world, I've learned." I forked a scallop as the plate made its way to me. "And here I thought we were just going to enjoy dinner together."

"There's no such thing as downtime with these guys," Seven murmured, grabbing a piece of bread from the bowl being passed.

"South America sounds exciting," Mercedes said with a grin. "Trace and I went to Chile last year for a wine tour. It was incredible."

"Only drank Petit Verdot for four days," Trace chimed in.

I took a quick sip of beer, more than ready to return to the most pressing matter at hand: what Mercedes had been about to tell me. "That sounds fancy. Mercedes, what were you in the middle of telling me before Nash showed up?"

She shook her head, waving it off. "It was nothing. If you're going to be starting something with the Nightingales, I don't want to interfere—"

"It's no bother," I reassured her, even though I had no idea what she'd been about to suggest. I just knew that it was attached to Maddie. "Is everything okay?"

Mercedes sighed, crumpling slightly. "Technically, yes? I just...I'm worried about Maddie."

Now we were getting somewhere. "Tell me more."

"She's been back in Louisville for the last few weeks, and she's been having some issues getting my brother to finalize the divorce." She drew a measured breath, gnawing on the inside of her cheek as she cut a scallop in half with her fork. "I'm worried things might get ugly. I have a feeling Jericho isn't going to make it easy on her."

Jericho, Mercedes's brother, was now Maddie's ex. I'd heard him mentioned once during my conversation with Maddie, but she didn't linger there, and I got no details other than he was the father of Maddie's daughter Grace, who had also joined her in New York City for the holidays. A fist formed in my gut as the pieces started to click together.

"Has Jericho been violent in the past?"

Mercedes's throat bobbed. "Manipulative is probably a better word. He has a knack for playing dirty. He was the one who originally broke me and Trace up when we first dated a decade ago, though I never found out until years later. And then Trace experienced Jericho's ways firsthand when he was staying in Louisville a year and a half ago. My brother will ruin your life without laying a finger on you."

"Sounds like a winner." I frowned down at my plate, suddenly not hungry. I didn't like knowing this about Maddie's ex. Now I was dying to do something about it.

"He's horrible. I can't wait until we no longer share the same last name. He and I haven't spoken for over a year and I have no intentions to change that."

"How'd you come out so nice?"

She laughed bitterly. "Don't you know? Southern girls are supposed to be sweet. Southern boys just take what they want."

I took another pull at my beer and cleared my throat. "It doesn't sound like Maddie is safe around him."

"I don't think anybody is safe around him. Jericho's been getting more erratic, based on what I've heard from Maddie. And that's what makes me scared." Mercedes paused to tend to Willow, who asked for help—and it could only be from Mercedes—with drinking her lemonade. When Willow was satisfied, Mercedes turned back to me. "Anyway, I was going to see if you had plans to go anywhere near there and convince you to make a pit stop and check in on her. But it sounds like you've set your plans now, so I'll see about sending someone else—"

"I am heading that way, actually."

Her green eyes widened. "Oh. You are?"

"Yeah." I wracked my brain to think about who in my network was in that area. Who could I call up or pretend to visit? "I'd planned to visit my friend's cabin after my gig here ended. Even with the

Nightingale offer, I can still do that. I'm pretty sure his cabin is in northern Kentucky somewhere."

She clutched at the sides of her face. "Oh my goodness. This is perfect! I thought it would be a long shot, so I almost didn't ask."

I didn't tell her that I'd rent a cabin if I had to, just to make sure Maddie was safe. My protectiveness didn't make sense to me. I'd spent a total of eight hours with Maddie and her daughter Grace, yet I'd said goodbye to her that night feeling like I was leaving my wife behind. I didn't form connections like that, the type where it felt destiny was somehow at work. The connections I had usually involved a dating app, one night, and zero follow-up.

But Maddie was different. From the second I saw her, I felt like I'd known her for years. And I couldn't say why.

"I'd be happy to check in on her," I told Mercedes.

And I meant it with every cell of my being.

Here was my chance to see if that connection with Maddie had been a holiday fluke.

CHAPTER TWO
MADDIE

"Mommy! Mommy!"

Grace, my blonde bundle of joy, rushed toward me as I pushed through the front door of my parents' house in east Louisville. I opened my arms to receive my daughter, coming down to my knees to give her a big hug.

This is how it went every day.

Say goodbye to her, practically in tears, around seven-thirty at the door of the preschool she attended, then see her beaming face first thing after work. Thankfully my mom was able to pick her up on days that I had to stay late at school, like today.

I had to thank my parents for *a lot* these days.

"I really missed you, Mommy." Her lisped words made my heart melt as our long hug went even longer. Tears pricked my eyes. How was I so lucky to have such a beautiful child? A child who loved me unreservedly, despite the ways I felt I'd failed her as her mother.

I tried not to let the dark thoughts swoop in. I'd been living with my parents for over a year since filing for divorce from Jericho. Removing him from Grace's daily life was a good thing. I tried to remind myself of this when I got too down on myself for being a divorcee raising a child in her parents' home.

"I missed you too, pumpkin." I kissed the top of Grace's head, finally releasing her from the hug. When I stood, Grace beamed up at me and reached for my hand. "What do you think we should have for dinner tonight?"

Grace loved to help plan dinner. In fact, she was my right-hand girl in all areas of life, from selecting my outfits to prepping meals to organizing the craft area. That didn't mean she was aways *helpful*, of course, but she loved to try. And despite all the pain and uncertainty that my separation from her father had brought to our lives, part of me felt that I was living in paradise at the same time.

For the first time in a *long* time, I knew what freedom tasted like.

Even if I wasn't fully free from Jericho yet, I was so close.

All he needed to do was sign the divorce papers, and that chapter of my life would be done. Per Kentucky law, we had to be separated for a full year before the formal divorce could go through. And we'd hit that milestone late last year. Jericho always had an excuse for why he hadn't finished his side of things. Logistically, it was simple, but Jericho was dragging his heels. I suspected it had to do with his not wanting to hash out a custody agreement or the division of our marital assets. At least, that was what my lawyer said. It was extra frustrating when we were so close to the finish line. Still, I chose to focus on the positives.

"I think we make sketti," she said, accompanying me through the house as I dropped my tote bags from my day at the local elementary school, where I taught first grade. Luckily, even though Jericho had forced me to be a stay at home mom, it hadn't been too hard to reactivate my teaching license and get back into the swing of things once I left him. I'd missed it more than I ever let myself realize during the hellish five years at that man's side.

The only good things to come of those years? Grace. And my sister-in-law Mercedes.

Even after Jericho signed these dang papers and I was free of the Hendricks name, Mercedes would remain my soul sister.

In the kitchen, I found my mom chopping vegetables for a snack tray. Her gray-blonde hair was pulled back into a low ponytail, and her face lit up when she saw me.

"Hello, dear! You're just in time for party prep."

I smiled as we hugged. Having a soft place to land—at mom and dad's house—after the separation was something I thanked them for every day. Their penchant for casual get-togethers helped me feel like life had direction and purpose, especially in those early months when I'd been so adrift and confused.

"Where's the party tonight?" I checked my phone as Grace danced around us with excitement. It was almost six. My dad walked into the kitchen, humming to himself with some sort of air filter in his hand. One of the many random Dad Tasks he filled his evenings with. He paused to kiss the top of my head and continued on his way.

"We're heading to Jerry and Susan's house," she said, crunching into a baby carrot. "And I've already got Grace on board, because their little granddaughter June is coming to play tonight."

Grace squealed with excitement. "I want to play with June!"

I smiled down at her, relishing her enthusiasm. Her toothy grin. The way she twirled her lavender skirt, which I could barely get her out of, she loved it so much. Sometimes I wasn't sure I could handle her being *any* cuter.

But going to Jerry and Susan's house tonight was not exactly what I wanted to do. After the long work week, I was dying for some quiet time in the bath.

"When are you heading over?" I reached for a broccoli floret.

She looked at her wristwatch, then resumed cutting. "In about twenty minutes."

"Oh jeez." I sighed, trying to imagine if I could scrounge up any energy for *more* socialization. After wrangling six- and seven-year-olds all day, plus finishing up all my work so I could fully clock out this weekend, I wasn't sure I could do much more than change out of work clothes and vegetate.

"I know what that sigh means," my mom said, waving the knife in my direction. "And I'll be honest—I won't be mad if you don't go."

My shoulders slumped, an unexpected weight releasing from them. "You won't?"

"I think you should have a night to yourself. It's Friday. Go see a movie or something."

I grabbed a slice of bell pepper and dipped it into the ranch dressing she'd just opened. "By myself?"

"You're in your independent woman era. Didn't you just tell me that the other day?"

"Well, yeah..." I munched thoughtfully, running my fingers through Grace's silky blonde tresses. "I guess there are a few frontiers I haven't explored yet."

"You can go to the movies by yourself. Go shopping by yourself. Heck, you can even go out for dinner by yourself!" The knife *thwacked* against the cutting board as she cut into the final head of broccoli.

"We having sketti?" Grace asked, looking up at me. I cupped her heart-shaped face in my hands and planted a kiss on her forehead.

"Well, it sounds like you and Grandma have plans." As I spoke, I began to visualize what I might most enjoy for tonight. I thought it had been a bath, but now I was seeing something else: slightly upscale restaurant. Sitting at the bar by myself. Maybe even reading a book at the bar. A thrill of excitement raced up my spine. My plan was cemented. "You're going to go play with June, and I bet they'll have some yummy dinner over there."

"Burgers," Mom said.

"With cheese?" Grace asked.

"All the cheese you could ask for," she confirmed with a final *thwack.*

The knife was the signal. Our Friday evenings were set, and mine looked a lot more exciting than I'd originally planned. I ran up to my room to get changed. This felt like a date night with myself, which was appropriate, given the transformation I'd undergone over the last year and few months.

I'd spent the first six months post-separation in transition mode: move out of the house I'd shared with Jericho; figure out how to renew my teaching license; start the job hunt; begin a new life under my parents' roof while saving up for a down payment. The last nine months had been more about starting to relax a little. Settling in. Navigating my way out of "married" status.

Things were going well—at least, as well as I could hope for.

Maybe tonight you'll even see a cute guy or two.

Something strange pinged inside me. It felt like longing, a deep, core-shaking kind. My mind instantly flitted to Troy, the man I'd met during my holiday trip to New York City. Grace and I had gone to visit Mercedes and Willow and Trace—and by extension, the entire Fairchild clan—and met a man I still couldn't forget.

I smiled to myself as I shed my dark slacks and puffy, cream sweater. Troy and I had only shared one long evening together at the Fairchild Christmas party a few weeks ago. It had been full of happy conversation, Willow and Grace chasing each other around the apartment, and such top-tier catering that I still hadn't been able to stop thinking about the filet mignon. Everyone else called him Trojan there, but when I tried to do the same, he stopped me. "I like it better when you call me by my real name," he'd said, and just remembering the rough scrape of his voice could still knock the wind out of me.

I thought about that man far too often to be considered sane. Maybe this was just the lonely life of a divorcee now. I bit at my bottom lip, recalling the tiny details I'd loved most about him: the scruff on his jawline, the heat that had poured off of him, the way he'd felt so strong and secure next to me. He was like a handsome bear, and from the second I'd met him, I wanted more of him.

But you won't get more. He's in New York, and you're here. Besides, what would he want with a single mom?

I frowned as I reached for a pair of jeans, shimmying into them before checking the fit in the stand-up mirror. I remembered suddenly I hadn't checked my phone in awhile. I fished it out of my purse, the screen lighting up with missed messages.

JERICHO: So are you planning on coming by with Grace anytime soon?

JERICHO: You could at least answer me.

JERICHO: Do you have to be such a bitch?

JERICHO: Forget it. Don't bring her over. But you and I need to square some things away right now.

Any good mood I'd cobbled together fell away. Jericho had a bad habit of being a completely unpredictable co-parent. He'd disappear for two full weeks, and then show up demanding a full weekend with Grace. That wasn't happening on my watch. Not when he'd been growing increasingly agitated by the smallest things.

I drew a deep breath, looking through my clothes in the closet. I needed something with long sleeves, thanks to Jericho. My forearm still throbbed from my visit earlier that week. I'd taken Grace to visit him and his parents at their house—a neutral area, or so I'd thought. Jericho had gotten so agitated about the divorce papers *yet again* that he'd yanked on my arm as I tried to hurry out the door, bringing me crashing into him, nearly clipping my chin on the doorway. Grace hadn't seen it, thank God. But the bruises he left behind were more than visible. And I didn't want anyone to see them.

Not Grace. Not my parents. Not even myself.

They were just a reminder of a phase of life I wanted behind me.

I opted for a loose fitting boho shirt with long, wide sleeves and a V-neck. Feminine but modest. I gathered my purse and a new paperback, and set off for the kitchen to say goodbye to Grace and my parents. Once I was out the door, snug in my puffy winter coat, the crisp winter air gave me a surge of energy.

This was my night out. Who knew what fun I might find? I headed for a trendy-looking bar and restaurant I found from a quick internet search. Someplace new and hip. Perfect for a single mom like me trying to begin the next chapter of her life. I sang to myself as I blasted Taylor Swift on my drive downtown, trying to ignore the way my phone kept lighting up with incoming texts.

JERICHO: Do you not know how to use a phone?

JERICHO: Wow. Just went to your parents' house and nobody's home.

JERICHO: Are you trying to keep my daughter from me? Answer me.

I pulled into the parking lot of the restaurant, my stomach doing flips. I didn't know why Jericho wouldn't just let me go. Custodial arrangements for Grace was one thing; this weird control he kept trying to exert over me was entirely different. I stuck to my guns when this sort of thing cropped up, enforcing boundaries I'd never had while we were married. But something behind his texts tonight had me worried.

Just go enjoy your night. Don't think about him anymore.

I hurried through the car-cluttered parking lot, pushing into the warm, fragrant air of the trendy brewpub. A hostess led me to a seat at the bar per my request, and as I slid onto the barstool, I received an image from Mercedes showcasing a gourmet dish with squirts of lavender and green on the edges of the plate...and not much else.

MADDIE: Wow that looks fancy. Is that what they're calling dinner for two these days?

MERCEDES: Trace's non-profit is hosting a gala and this is the appetizer. I'm about to lick the plate. Pregnant and starving.

MADDIE: Don't be uncouth. Get a very dainty spoon.

I snapped a picture of the bar and sent it to her.

MADDIE: I'll be ordering my dinner from here soon.

MERCEDES: I'm glad you're out doing something. Has everything been okay? Be honest.

MADDIE: Your brother is making things hard. He won't stop texting today.

MERCEDES: Where are you?

MADDIE: Some new place called Espuma. It's a girls' night out for one. I'm trying something you'd approve of: reading at the bar.

MERCEDES: Sounds fun. I'd totally read at the bar next to you. How long do you plan on staying?

I frowned down at my phone. Her questions about my location were odd, but maybe she was making a joke. Ever since she'd started dating Trace Fairchild, she'd become a type of *bon vivant* who wasn't afraid to take his private jet across the country for the right reason, but flying out to join me seemed a little impractical.

MADDIE: I just got here. Are you going to surprise me for my solo girl's night?

MERCEDES: Surprise, yes. Me? No.

She wouldn't give up more information despite my repeated texts, but I didn't have long to wonder. The bartender approached for my drink and food order, which I gave him—pinot grigio, a basket of bread with olive oil dip, salmon with rice. I pulled my paperback out of my purse once he'd hurried away to the next customer, intent on fulfilling this fantasy of reading at a bar.

I was barely two pages in when the energy crackled. Hairs on my forearms stood up, and I set down my book, looking around. The restaurant was raucous and busy, but despite all the moving bodies and loud chatter, something snagged my attention from across the room.

Dark chestnut hair, long enough to run your fingers through. Broad shoulders, almost like boulders, stretching a dark coat to its limits. His brown eyes surveyed the restaurant methodically until they landed on me. Warmth spread through me.

Troy.

A smile curled his lips. I lifted my hand, unsure if I was imagining him. The only thing that kept me from acting as though this was a hallucination was the fact that Mercedes had told me I'd be surprised.

This was beyond surprise.

This was a dream come true.

"Troy?" I couldn't contain the shocked laughter that cascaded out of me as he crossed the space between us in powerful steps. When he reached my side, he towered over me. I held out my arms for a hug.

"Maddie. Good to see you." His deep voice at my ear was like a salve. My eyes fluttered shut as he pulled me into a warm, healing hug that smelled like cedar and man. A satisfied hum escaped me, and I lingered in his embrace for a few moments too long. He made it hard to want to disconnect.

"Oh, gosh. You too," I said once he finally released me. I wobbled back into my seat at the bar, and he slid into the empty seat next to me. Was this really happening? "What are you doing here?"

His jaw flexed as he faced me at the bar, his jean-clad knees knocking mine. A mischievous grin tugged at his perfect lips. "Just passing through. Thought I'd say hi."

"You talked to Mercedes about this, didn't you?" I pushed my paperback away, opting instead for a sip of the wine that had just arrived.

"Maybe." He tipped his head, that same warmth and familiarity from the Christmas party returning in full force. It was like no time at all had passed. "How you been?"

Three simple words that opened up a flood gate of emotion. I drew a shaky breath, not sure where to begin. "Is it possible to say both 'I've been better' and 'This is the best time of my life'?"

"You can say whatever you want to, and I'll believe it."

His simple words landed like a hammer. Paired with the mischief curling at his lips and the scent of him infiltrating my senses, I felt like I was falling head first into the abyss. I'd wanted Troy from the second I laid eyes on him, and here he was. Right in front of me.

Where will this lead us?

"I'm not sure you should give me so much power," I teased Troy, setting my glass of wine back on the bar. "There could be consequences."

His gaze darkened slightly, and he wet his bottom lip as he leaned imperceptibly closer. "I think I'm ready to handle them."

I rolled my lips inward, trying to stave off the girlish giggles that threatened to spill out of me. Was this real life? I'd been thinking of this man non-stop for the past three weeks. I toyed with the stem of my wine glass, dragging my gaze up to his. We smiled at each other for a moment, the silence between us comfortable. As though we'd known each other for decades already.

Why has it felt so easy with him from day one?

"Are you here to eat?" I asked him, then realized what a dumb question that was for someone who had just come into a restaurant.

"Was hoping maybe we could get a weird cheese plate," he said. The excitement that bubbled up in me was immediate. I *loved* weird cheese. And then I remembered we'd talked about weird cheeses in New York. And then I realized—*he'd remembered.* Why was that so touching?

"You came all the way from New York to get a weird cheese plate with me?" I couldn't keep the skepticism from my voice.

"Maybe. I'm definitely ready to eat." His cheek twitched as he said that, and the way his chin dipped had me thinking of him eating something else entirely. A blush warmed my cheek as I pushed the menu toward him, rattling off what I'd ordered only minutes prior. When I was done regaling him with my order, a movement over his shoulder caught my attention. The flash of a jawline that seemed too familiar. Blond hair that gleamed under the lights.

Across the restaurant, at the front door, Jericho had walked in.

Everything inside me seized. I must have looked stricken because Troy narrowed his eyes at me, leaning closer.

"Maddie?"

I swallowed hard, unable to move my gaze from Jericho. He wasn't alone. He'd come with friends—specifically Caleb, his best friend from college, and two others who tended to follow him blindly. Their gazes moved across the restaurant, seeking something.

Was it me?

Panic swirled inside me. I didn't want Jericho to see me. He *couldn't.* But I didn't know how to escape or how to blend in. So I did the only thing that seemed available.

I leaned into Troy.

In the back of my mind, I thought I might be able to hide myself behind his broad shoulders, using him as a shield. But the closer I got to him, the harder I panicked. My brain stopped communicating with my torso. My limbs jerked awkwardly, and my body followed the only path forward that made sense: kissing Troy.

Our lips connected softly. The warmth of him was the first thing I noticed, the way his heat and cedar trickled through me, down to my cells. I could sense his surprise, but more than that, I sensed his compliance. His big, rough hands caught my elbows as I leaned into him.

Troy didn't pull away. He only deepened the kiss, his lips parting, inviting my tongue to meet his. What had started as an accidental kiss now turned into something so much more. *This* was intentional. It was fucking *hot*.

He traced the edge of my bottom lip with his tongue, one kiss bleeding into another. By the time I pulled away from him, I couldn't even remember how the kiss had started. I blinked up at him, fully dazed. The same expression greeted me in return.

Desire pooled in his eyes, and he ran this thumb back and forth over the crook of my elbow where he still held me.

"That was a nice way to say hello," he murmured, his voice gritty. "Is that how you greet everyone you haven't seen in awhile?"

"I'm sorry," I started, but had nothing to follow up with.

"Don't be." He squeezed my arms, tipping his head as he watched me. "Do you know how long I've been wanting to do that?"

My eyes widened in surprise. "Are you serious?"

A movement over his shoulder caught my eye, bringing me crashing back to the present. Tension still tugged at the edges of this unexpectedly romantic moment. Jericho and his friends were crossing the restaurant. Coming this way. I turned away from Troy, facing the bar, and reached up to tighten my ponytail.

"What's this?" Troy's voice had an edge to it. I glanced over at him, finding his brows wrought in concern. He reached for my exposed forearm. My loose sleeves had slid back while I adjusted my hair, revealing the mottled bruising from my run-in with Jericho the other night.

I swallowed hard, slipping the sleeves back down. I glanced over Troy's shoulder, shrinking. "I don't...it's just..."

"Is this from your ex?"

I didn't know what to say. So I nodded.

The last vestige of a smile faded from Troy's face.

CHAPTER THREE

TROY

ALL OF THE SEXY time thoughts I'd been having after that kiss faded away when I put the pieces together.

Mercedes had been wrong. Her brother was a fucking abuser.

Anger licked through my veins. Sure, I'd love to kiss Maddie a thousand times over. But seeing this—bruises left behind by a weak man, the fear flitting through her eyes—had me only thinking about fucking up her ex.

"He got upset," she said quietly, her gaze occasionally darting over my shoulder, as though keeping an eye on something. "I took Grace over to see him at his parents' house after we got back from New York. But he didn't like that we didn't stay long. And then he started bitching about the whole entire trip to New York. When I tried to leave, well..."

I balled my hands into fists beneath the bar. When she looked across the room one more time, I asked, "What is it? Is he here?"

She nibbled on her bottom lip, nodding. Her gaze remained stuck on some point past my shoulder. "He just showed up with Mercedes' ex-fiancé, Caleb, and two of their friends."

She picked nervously at a cuticle while she gnawed at her lip. I angled myself toward her, reaching for the worrying hand. "Hey. You're with me. You're safe."

Her hazel eyes connected with mine in a spark as she nodded. "Yeah. You're right. And we're in public, so..."

"Will you show me which one he is? Who did this to you?"

"He's the one with the blue jacket." Her voice came out a whisper. I twisted to look behind me, barely able to pick them out across the restaurant. A group of men sat at a table in the middle of the room, but one glance at their faces told me they hadn't come for a meal. They were here to find *her*.

Maybe they'd already spotted her. Maybe they just knew she was somewhere inside. Either way, I didn't want to take the chance.

"Let's get out of here," I said, reaching for her hand. I swiped my thumb back and forth, hoping to console her. She didn't know it yet, but she had no reason to worry while I was with her. I had no problem taking down four douchebrothers in full view of the public. I'd gotten myself into—and out of—far dicier situations than this one. And from the looks of it, her ex Jericho would crumble with one well-placed punched to his nose.

Maddie's worried gaze searched my face. "I didn't even get my food yet."

"We'll go somewhere else," I promised her. "I just need you far away from that guy."

"Okay," she said, but she didn't look convinced. I leaned forward, cupping the side of her face in my hand.

"What did I tell you before? You're with me. You're safe."

She rolled her lips in, nodding. "He's just a piece of work. He and Caleb ruined Mercedes' life. He barred Mercedes from going to their grandmother's funeral. He and Caleb sent bomb threats..." Her voice broke and she shook her head. "I don't want you getting involved—"

"Too late," I said with a smile. "You kissed me. I'm involved. And for what it's worth, a bomb threat isn't enough to get me to back down. Now, are you ready?"

A small smile curled at her pretty pink lips. It was a small sign of progress, at least. I held her small hand in mine, surging to my feet. I was now the human shield between her and those idiots.

I dropped a $100 bill on the counter and led the way toward the door, keeping her close to my side. Given where the men sat, it was impossible to hide her fully without drawing even more attention. I kept an eye on the guys as we navigated through the crowded restaurant. Her ex scanned the room with a dark, shifty gaze. He just looked like he was up to no good.

We slipped out the door, leaving the dull roar of conversation behind. Outside, the crisp, late January air prickled through my lungs. I wrapped an arm around her slight shoulders as we walked to the parking lot.

"Do you want to go somewhere else? So you can get that dinner you were waiting on."

"Yeah..." Her face fell. "I hate that he ruined this. I know it probably sounds like a pity party, but I'd been looking forward to this place." She huffed as we approached what I assumed was her car, a simple silver sedan. She paused by the trunk, pulling something out of her purse. "I was telling Mercedes that all I wanted to do was go someplace nice and read this book at the bar by myself."

"Then that's what we'll do. Except I'm coming with you. I don't trust that prick. So just think of me as a mute companion. I won't even talk to you so you can read."

She grinned up at me, a dimple in her left cheek flashing. That pretty grin and the wisps of brown hair escaping from her ponytail had me ready to follow her wherever she wanted to go, for however long she'd let me. I stepped closer, reaching for her hand again. It was a natural move, one that felt more intimate than protective.

"My paperback bodyguard?"

"Something like that." I reached up to cup the side of her face but caught myself before I could. She'd kissed me out of sheer panic, that didn't mean she wanted me moving in for more. It was too easy to play that part with her though; I'd felt the pull the second I met her.

But I didn't want to think about that right now. I was here to make sure she stayed safe. Then I was heading to Ecuador to hopefully start the next chapter of my life.

"*Maddie!*" The rough bark of a male voice cut through the night air.

She gasped as her gaze connected with somebody behind me. I didn't need to guess who it was. I turned to find Jericho storming out of the restaurant, his three friends close behind.

I registered the most important things first: the aggression leaking out of his closed fists. The fire in his eyes. The speed with which he approached us. All of these were signs to get Maddie to safety.

"Maddie, get in my car." I fished my key fob out of my pocket and clicked to unlock. "Black Jeep, two spots down."

She opened her mouth to say something but then nodded and hurried off.

"Why you running?" Jericho taunted, course correcting to follow her. I strode behind her, angling my path so I'd intersect Jericho before he reached my Jeep. "Just want to have a conversation with my wife, is that too much to goddamn ask?"

My steps thudded on the asphalt as I intercepted Jericho's path. He barreled right into me, so laser-focused on Maddie that I wasn't even sure he'd seen me yet. His green eyes snapped up to me, brows a hard line across his face. In my peripheral vision, I saw Maddie slam the door shut. *Success.*

"And who the fuck are you?" Jericho's voice came out rimmed with knives. He had to tip his head back to look up at me, bless his heart, but that didn't stop him from puffing out his chest. His friends came to a stop behind him like the good little minions they were.

"Doesn't matter. All I know is that you're a nuisance, and you need to step away."

Jericho's eyes narrowed, a bonafide creepy smirk tugging at his lips. "She's my wife. I think *you're* the one who needs to step away." He called out toward the Jeep, "Is this who you've been cheating on me with? You're probably knocked up already, aren't you?"

The slur in his voice was subtle. But the whiskey wind coming from his mouth was not. I rolled my neck in a slow circle, sizing up my possible plans of attack.

"I'm going to ask you one more time to leave," I said succinctly. I held his gaze, not missing the way he signaled something to one of the friends. The dark-haired one peeled off, hurrying away to a nearby SUV.

"I'm pretty sure you don't get to decide who's in this public parking lot," Jericho said with a sneer.

"Maybe so. But there's one thing I do get to decide," my voice was nearly a growl as I stepped forward, erasing the distance between us as I used my full height on him, "and that's whether you ever lay a hand on Maddie again."

From the corner of my eye, I saw his friend returning to the group. But this time, he had a baseball bat in his hands.

It was cute how he thought that would be enough to scare me away.

"From here on out," I spat out, "if you see Maddie, expect to see me too."

A bitter laugh escaped him, but I could tell he was struggling to keep his confidence. When I stepped forward again, he stepped back.

"You don't fucking scare me," Jericho said. "And if you come one step closer, we'll make sure you can't walk out of here."

His tone pushed me over the edge; or maybe it was the flash of remembering the fingerprint bruises I'd found up and down Maddie's forearms. Whatever it was, I'd had enough of looking at his sorry face. I snagged Jericho by the collar of his coat, bringing him closer so that I could deliver a swift punch to his rib cage.

I moved so fast he didn't have time to respond, but his friends reacted.

"You're gonna regret that," the one with the baseball bat said before he swung. He hit me in the hip, a dull *thwup* that didn't register at first but I was sure I'd feel later. For now, it only irritated me. I had inches on all these guys and the panic in their eyes told me I had far more experience in various types of combat than they did put together.

While Jericho gasped for breath, I lunged for the guy with the baseball bat. He got one more hit on me, aiming for the back of my knees but clipping my left kneecap instead. *Ouch.* I grabbed the bat before he could hit me again, ripping it out of his hands.

"Get the fuck out of here now before I bash all of your dumbass skulls in," I growled, stepping forward. My knee screamed with pain, but now wasn't the time to think about a potential injury. I towered over them. Jericho backed up, glaring at me as his friends retreated alongside him.

"Have a great night," I called out jovially, popping on a big ol' sarcastic smile. "Thanks for the new sporting equipment, pals."

"Shut the fuck up," Jericho snarled.

"It's been a real pleasure," I went on.

They grumbled further, piling into their SUV. I watched as they peeled out of the parking lot, only smiling and waving as they pelted me with middle fingers through the safety of their rolled up windows. I popped the baseball bat in the backseat of the Jeep, and then slid into the driver's seat. Maddie had her face buried in her hands, her whole body shaking.

"Hey. They're gone." I reached across the console to wrap an arm around her shoulders. "You okay?"

She sniffed, dragging her head up. "I should be asking *you* that question! Troy, he hit you!"

"It was a love tap," I said, though I knew that was false. My knee burned while bent, and that wasn't a good sign.

Her shoulders hitched with a sob. "This is so messed up. I'm so sorry. I-I didn't want for any of this to happen. I just wanted to come out for a nice meal—"

"Hey. This isn't your fault. You're not the one chasing dudes with a baseball bat. *He* is. There's nothing for you to apologize for."

She looked at me with red-rimmed eyes, sadness pouring out of her. "You don't have to be doing this."

"I want to make sure you're safe." I reached for her hand, giving it a squeeze. "That's all I care about."

"Thank you. I don't know what I would have done without you, Troy."

"You're welcome, Maddie." My chest swelled, reminding me of the persistent ache that throbbed there. While I was aware of how much I cared for Maddie, pretty much from the second I laid eyes on her, I didn't know how to process it. My life didn't have room for someone like Maddie. "Where should we head to next? Plan B dinner?"

"I'm not even hungry anymore. He scared the hunger right out of me." She rubbed her forehead. "I guess I should go back to my parents' house. I just hope he doesn't show up there again. He was sending me angry texts earlier about how I wasn't at my mom and dad's house when he stopped by."

My insides tightened at her words. Multiple alarms were going off inside me, and I wasn't sure if she realized how dangerous this guy could get.

"I don't think you'll be safe at your parents' house either." The bodyguard in me was already hatching a protection plan. And it involved me staying glued to her side. "It sounds like his behavior has been escalating. He went from manipulative to leaving bruises to showing up with a gang of friends with baseball bats. Maddie, I know he's Grace's dad...but this guy is officially a threat."

She drew a deep breath, her chin trembling.

"I know it's not what you want to hear, but we need to get you out of here. Someplace *safe*."

"But where?" Her voice sounded so small, so afraid.

I started the Jeep, enjoying the rumble of the engine.

Lucky for her, I had a plan.

CHAPTER FOUR
MADDIE

"You don't have to agree to this," Troy started as he backed out of the parking spot, "but I'd like to personally escort you to your parents' house so you can pack some things for a little trip. Grace, too."

"A *trip*?" Now hardly seemed like the time for a vacation.

"After what I've seen, I don't think you're safe staying without personal protection." He paused in the parking lot as he switched to drive, but he didn't move forward. Instead, he looked over at me. "It's your choice. But I'm recommending three thousand percent that you get out of town so we can develop a security plan without him on our asses. A friend of mine has a cabin just outside of town that we can use. It's far enough away that he won't be able to find us. There's no risk of him ruining another meal."

My head spun. I'd gone from normal divorcee to the subject in a bad breakup film. Jericho's friends were busting people with baseball bats now? Nothing made sense. Except for Troy.

He made a *lot* of sense. His even-keeled, calm demeanor, even in the face of danger, felt like a warm, flickering fire in the middle of a cold night. I wanted to cozy up next to him and stay as long as he'd let me.

"I-I can't just up and leave..."

He nodded, the first flash of doubt crossing his face. He looked genuinely torn as he studied the other cars in the parking lot.

"Do your parents have a spare room?" he asked.

I laughed, but I could tell he wasn't joking.

"I've seen a lot, Maddie." His throat bobbed as he looked over at me. The dim glow from the lights in the parking lot illuminated the handsome features of his face. His dark eyes drank me in, and for a moment the rest of the world fell away. "He's upgraded to leaving marks on you. He showed up at a restaurant with friends ready to beat somebody down. And they tried. If I'd been anyone else who didn't know how to handle the situation, I'd probably be headed to the ER right now. Based on his current behavior, I wouldn't put it past him to hurt you—or Grace—next."

His words sank into me, bringing the fear back to the forefront. I'd never worried that he'd hurt me, or Grace. But now? After tonight? I could see it happening. Even though I wanted to believe that he was ready to quietly accept the divorce and move on with his life.

"I'm sorry," he said quietly, reaching for my hand again. He stroked it like we'd been together for years—not like we were two technical strangers. That was the dizzying affect Troy had on me. "I don't mean to upset you. But this is the reality of the situation, and you need to know. This is part of my job."

I nodded, allowing the truth to settle inside me. I was no longer in *normal breakup territory* with Jericho. He'd pushed it into something sinister and scary. "You're right. I'll go back to my parents' house and get things packed up." I reached for the door handle, but he grabbed my wrist.

"I'll drive. I don't want you out of my sight right now."

I sank back into the seat, his words warming me. He rolled into motion, and I gave him directions on how to maneuver through Louisville to my parents' house. I had him wait in the car in the driveway, partly as a way so I could get my bearings. Was I really about to run away with this man I hardly knew? Surely I would be fine here with my mom and dad.

But maybe I didn't *want* to spend the next few days without Troy.

I called Mercedes as I hurriedly packed my and Grace's things. She answered on the third ring.

"Is everything okay?" she asked.

"As okay as it can be, considering your unhinged brother." We tried to make it a joke that she was related to him, but the soft sigh told me the joke hadn't landed like it normally did.

"I was worried about that. Is Trojan there with you?"

"He is. He intercepted Jericho and Caleb and two of their friends in the parking lot outside the restaurant. They brought a baseball bat and Troy took a couple blows. But he scared them off and now we're heading out of town."

"Oh my God. You were right about the unhinged part. Where are you guys heading?"

"I don't know yet. It's some place Troy suggested." I nibbled on my lip as I assessed the quick suitcase I'd thrown together. "Am I crazy to go with him? We're going to pick up Grace once I get everything packed."

"Honestly? No. I'd trust that man with my life. He and Seven are the smartest, most trustworthy men I've ever met." Mercedes added off to the side, "Of course except for *you*, Bear. I'm talking to Maddie about bodyguards."

I laughed softly. "Tell him not to worry, we all know he's your number one."

"Now that I'm pregnant he's extra territorial," she said with a little giggle.

"Believe me, I noticed." I zipped my suitcase, cradling the phone between my ear and shoulder. "Well, as long as you don't think I'm crazy for running off into the night with a man like Troy, then I think that's what I'm about to do."

"That man helped save Trace and his brothers from prison time. Trust me when I say: you have the green light, from *all* of us here in New York."

I hung up the phone and pocketed it, feeling a particular sort of sadness. Part of me wanted to be back in New York too. But it just didn't seem possible. My entire life was in Kentucky. What reason would I have for moving to New York that made any ounce of sense?

Maybe just because you want to.

I pushed the thoughts away, checking the bedroom one final time to make sure I hadn't forgotten anything important for Grace or myself. As soon as I stepped out the front door, Troy practically tumbled out of the car to relieve me from the hassle of the suitcase.

"I'll take this," he said, easily plucking it from me.

I thanked him and slipped into the passenger side of the Jeep, thinking about our next steps when I realized something important: we didn't have Grace's booster seat. It was still in my car at the restaurant. Once Troy was back in the driver's seat, I told him, "I made a major mistake. I forgot to grab Grace's booster, and we need it for her to ride in the car. Can we go back?"

My insides clenched waiting for his response. All I could hear was Jericho's voice in my head: *what a fucking waste of time! Why didn't you think of this before? You couldn't have told me before?*

Instead of echoing what I heard in my head, Troy just nodded. "Of course. That's easy."

I let out a breath I hadn't realized I'd been holding. Such simple words that dissolved my anxiety. Did he realize how helpful he was?

I looked over at him, watching the shadows shift across his face as we drove through traffic. "Thanks, Troy." Thanks wasn't strong enough of a word, but I wasn't sure how to convey to him just how grateful I was.

He cast me an easy grin. "It's my pleasure, Maddie."

The drive back to the restaurant was unnaturally quick, likely due to all the thoughts careening through my head. When we pulled into the parking lot, he swore under his breath as he slowed to a stop behind my car.

"That fucker," he muttered.

"What?"

"Look at your tires."

I connected the dots as he was saying the words. My car sat lower than normal, thanks to the four slashed tires it now sported. I covered my mouth as I stared out the window.

"He's never gone this far before," I whispered.

"Even more reason for you and Grace to not to be anywhere he might be able to find you." He sighed heavily, putting the car into park. "Is the booster in the back seat? I'll go grab it, just unlock the door for me."

"I can get it—"

"Maddie." He sent me a stern look, but the corners of his lips curled. "You gotta know by now that while you're with me, you're not lifting a finger."

I fished my keys out of my purse and clicked the car to unlock, biting back a little smile as he headed for the backseat and tugged the booster out. Something in his gait looked off; I studied him as closely as I could but he was back to the Jeep before I could make a determination.

"You ready for this jelly?"

"If the jelly is runaway-flavored, I guess so."

He cracked a heartbreaker grin as he rolled into motion. "I'll be honest, I wasn't expecting you to make a jelly flavor joke like that, and I'm not prepared with a good comeback. But just know, I'm much wittier in usual circumstances."

And just like that, even more of the tension of the night snapped. I grinned over at him, remembering how easily that night at Seven and Jordan's had disappeared for us. *Like this.*

"If you can't be level ten witty in the wake of being attacked by a guy with a baseball bat, then..." I drifted off, shaking my head. He looked like he was holding in laughter. "Then I think I'm going to have to runaway to someone else's cabin."

His shoulders shook with laughter. "Okay. I'll drop you off at another bodyguard's house."

Poking fun at the situation really helped to lessen some of the anxiety. The car ride progressed like that—banter tempered with questions from Grace and the occasional moments of easygoing silence.

"How does your leg feel?" I asked him.

He shrugged. "Fine. Why do you ask?"

"You took a baseball bat to the knee."

"Nah, I'm good."

"I don't believe you." That would explain the hint of a limp I'd seen. Or maybe I'd only *thought* I'd seen it. "That had to have hurt."

"I've experienced worse, I promise." He flashed me a smile that told me to drop it, because I wouldn't get the answer I wanted out of him. "You don't have to worry about me, Maddie."

"But maybe I want to?"

He looked over at me, and even in the darkness I could see the question marks in his gaze. There was something heavy behind my words that even I wasn't sure I'd intended. But there it was.

The truth of the matter.

If he'd chosen me to protect...then I could choose him to worry about.

Even though I wanted to do a lot more with him than just worry.

CHAPTER FIVE
TROY

"Where are we Mommy?"

Grace's little voice in the backseat of my Jeep felt like a spear to my heart. Nothing about this situation was right. The fact that they had to leave Louisville to feel safe; the fact that they even needed me to begin with. In a perfect world, Maddie would have married a guy who wasn't a level ten douchebag. But we didn't live in a perfect world...and maybe part of me was secretly glad that I was the one who was able to catch her when she needed the support.

"We're at the cabin I told you about when we left the party." Maddie's voice was a calming hush as she stroked her daughters' silk blonde hair. We were roughly forty five minutes outside of Louisville in a cabin owned by Len, one of my good friends, as a "safe house". Really he used it as an outpost on his cross-country security gigs—I had a lot of traveling bodyguards as friends—but it was also stocked as an emergency spot in case things went south politically or economically. He wasn't an apocalyptic nut, but he did have three years' worth of rations in the basement.

"Let's get you two inside." I headed for the back of the Jeep, ignoring the screaming pain in my knee. I needed to rest and I'd wake up fine—that was a demand more than a hope. I plucked Maddie's bag out of the back along with my own, the automatic lights of the sprawling wooden porch clicking on as I got closer to the front door.

"This place is pretty nice," Maddie murmured once she had Grace in her arms. The scraggly branches of the bare trees framed the edges of the cabin, which was nestled at the end of a long driveway in the forest. I set our bags at the front door as I wrestled with the lockbox to get it open. After inputting the wrong code about six times, I finally got the key out with a satisfied grunt. When I caught Maddie's eye, she was biting back a smile.

"What's so funny?"

"I love how you can defend me against four men but a little lockbox will take you out."

I snorted with amusement as I unlocked the door and pushed it open. Then I turned my gaze to her, lifting a brow.

"It didn't take me out," I told her. "And who won after all?" I flashed the glinting key.

Amusement shone in her eyes and we shared an electric moment. It was easy to get lost in her warm, hazel eyes. A little too easy.

"Mm hmm." She cast me a coy grin, one that I wanted to kiss off her face. I hoisted our bags and stepped inside, fumbling for the light switch. A moment later, the huge, open floor plan was illuminated by overhead lights. In the center of the room, dangling from the ceiling, Len had crafted a chandelier out of buckhorns. Not a hunting nut either, but he was abnormally fond of that chandelier. Maybe because he'd crafted the base out of spare dryer parts.

"Wow." Maddie's eyes widened as she looked around. It was a small, loft-style cabin: open plan kitchen and great room downstairs, with a small bedroom and bathroom off to the side. And then an open loft area upstairs. Everything reeked of wood and must, but in the good way.

"There's a bedroom right off to the side here." I led the way across the tiled floor of the kitchen, measuring my steps to hide the way my burning knee impacted my gait. The wheels of her bag clicked behind me until I pushed open the bedroom door and flicked the light on. The queen bed was thankfully made with a heavy blanket laid out on top. Grace snored softly in her mother's arms and barely roused when Maddie slid her onto the bed.

"Thank you." She sent me an appreciative look. "I'm going to get her tucked in and then...I think I'm going to head to bed too."

"You two rest up. I'll be out here if you need anything." I left her to unpack, knowing to my bones that space right now was the best idea. Not just because she was a single mom with a kid—but because if I looked at her for even a second longer, I'd be suggesting she find me in the loft that night.

Better to ignore those thoughts entirely. I got busy opening things up in the cabin, checking the water, lighting the fireplace, making sure everything was in good, working order. I'd be giving Len a full report—which started with a complementary picture of his favorite chandelier.

As I rummaged around the cabin, it was hard to keep my thoughts from sliding to Maddie. I had no business thinking about her in any sense other than a temporary protection gig. That's what this was, after all. Mercedes wanted me to check on her, so here I was. Nothing more, nothing less.

So I needed to focus on something else. Being that Len's cabin had no cable or internet, I had no interest in the huge TV in the great room. Instead, I got a small fire going in the fireplace to warm the place, and then headed to the loft to check my emails.

I'd gotten a notification during the drive that Nash Nightingale had emailed, but hadn't wanted to look until now. It was an itinerary—forwarded from someone else's email who seemed to be associated with a private jet company.

NYC to Quito, Ecuador.

Departure time, airport info, and a rough sequence of events once we landed in Ecuador. I scanned the information, feeling something in my gut tighten.

A week and a half away. Would that be enough time to get Maddie on stable ground?

She's not your responsibility. You're just helping out a friend. You'll ride out this phase and then get her set up with a basic protection plan.

It seemed so logical, so easy.

Which didn't explain why everything inside of me rejected the idea.

CHAPTER SIX

MADDIE

"Mommy, you smell dat?"

Grace's sweet voice roused me from my slumber. I squinted against the sunlight streaming in the slatted wood blinds, taking a moment to remember where the heck I was.

Log cabin. Kentucky wilderness. Safe with Troy.

The last part removed some deep tension between my shoulders. I snuggled into the covers, pulling Grace into my arms.

"Smells like breakfast, baby."

"Who cooking?"

"Probably Troy," I told her, stroking the white blonde hair framing her face. "Remember he brought us here? For our fun vacation."

She nodded, fidgeting in a way that told me she was dying to get out there and join the action.

"I wanna see," she said, voice bordering on a whine, when I didn't move.

"Okay sweetheart. Mommy will get up. We need to go brush teeth and do our hair first, okay?"

Grace rolled out of bed, hopping excitedly beside me as I sat up and stretched. I ushered her into the bathroom right across the hallway, catching the *pop-sizzle* of something cooking in the kitchen. We made quick work of getting ready for the day, complete with silly faces in the mirror and some butterfly kisses. On our way out of the bathroom, instead of heading back into the bedroom to change, Grace bolted into the kitchen.

"Good morning, you!" Troy's deep voice boomed through the cabin. I followed behind her, crossing my arms over my plain pink pajama set as I leaned against the doorway.

Troy wore gray sweatpants and a brown henley shirt, both of which were too sexy on him. I couldn't think too long about his thick forearms or the fact that gray sweatpants were one of the more erotic things a man could wear. And dammit, I would *not* look below his waistline. When he turned my way, his smile grew a little wider.

"And good morning, you." His gaze traveled from my toes to my head, and a small shiver traveled up my spine.

No, if I knew what was good for me, I'd just stop making eye contact with him from here on out. "Morning. Sure smells good out here."

Grace pulled out a stool at the big kitchen island, grunting as she struggled to get into the right spot. I helped her get on, trying not to ogle the beefy bodyguard cooking breakfast with a green dish towel tossed over his left shoulder.

"You two sleep okay?" The low rumble of his voice made my thighs clench.

"We slept wonderfully. How about you?"

He grunted and nodded. "I slept in for the first time in awhile. Until seven."

I glanced at the clock. It was almost eight thirty. "What have you been doing since seven?"

He flipped off the stove and tugged the towel from his shoulder, turning to me with a confident grin. "Squats. Sit-ups. Pushups. Things like that."

Electricity crackled between us as I beheld his full, beefy stature. Of course I immediately imagined him doing those things, even imagining what he might look like beneath that Henley. Forget never making eye contact again. I wanted to get lost in his brown eyes and never be found.

I blinked hard. *Snap out of it Maddie.*

"Mommy, I wanna color." Grace's pronunciation of 'color' sounded more like 'kuh-wor'; her little phonetic lilts always made my heart swell.

"You're ready for a coloring book sweetie?" I reached for the tote I'd placed on the island the night before. It had all of Grace's entertainment options for our trip—crayons, books, blank paper, and more. She squealed excitedly as I pulled out a nature coloring book along with a pack of crayons.

"I bet it's gonna be the prettiest picture," Troy said, pans clanking as he plated the food and put the cookware in the sink. A pile of scrambled eggs steamed from three separate plates, along with bacon and buttered wheat toast.

"I draw you!" Grace beamed up at him before beginning her masterpiece.

"Thanks for the breakfast," I told him, licking my lips as he set a plate in front of me and Grace. She only glanced at the eggs. She was a slow eater, especially when focused on a project. "I didn't realize our getaway included catering."

"All the amenities at Chateau Lenny," he said wryly before pulling out his own stool and plopping down. The wood groaned beneath his weight, but he didn't seem concerned about it. He dug into his eggs, something masculine even in the way he held his fork. I snapped my eyes back to my own plate, determined not to overanalyze the way he held a fork and somehow find a way to fawn over him.

I was a few bites into the eggs—fluffy, perfectly salted—when a text from my mom came in.

MOM: Good morning honey. I didn't want to worry you last night but you should know Jericho came by late last night, after we were in bed.

My stomach sank as soon as I saw the words.

"I guess it's a good thing we got out of town." I forked another bite of eggs. "My mom just texted that Jericho stopped by last night."

MOM: He pounded on the door until we got out of bed and answered. Wasn't too happy to hear you weren't there but we got him to leave.

My frown deepened.

"He didn't do anything, did he?"

"It doesn't seem like it. Got my parents out of bed though, which is a little rude." I sighed, pushing the eggs around my plate.

"Daddy coming?" Grace peered up at me, her pink crayon paused halfway across the sheet.

"No, sweetie. He's not." I stroked her hair, wondering what else I should add, if anything. She was too young to grasp what was going on, but she still noticed when things were off. She'd gotten used to the fact that Daddy didn't come around much, ever since we moved out of the house we used to share with Jericho. And maybe it was just me projecting, but...it didn't seem like she missed him. Maybe because he'd never spent much time with her to begin with.

"This is a Mommy and Grace vacation," Troy said, grinning down at her. "Just for you two."

She seemed satisfied with that answer so she went back to coloring.

"Speaking of vacation, where did these eggs and bacon come from?"

"I brought them with me from New York." Troy cocked a grin before he bit into a slice of bacon. "I had a cooler in the Jeep and the bacon was frozen. I wasn't sure what to expect at the cabin so I came stocked."

"Thanks for sharing your rations with us."

"I'll share my rations with you anytime, Maddie." His husky rasp made another wave of heat crash through me. The man could read cooking instructions and make it sound hot. "But I'll need to head to the store today if we want to have any more meals."

"Oh. A trip into town. That sounds fun."

He lowered his chin, narrowing his eyes. "I don't know if you should come."

"Oh, please. We're an hour from Louisville. I don't think Jericho has any idea where I am, nor will we run into him at the store." Despite my protests, his protective mode was a turn-on.

He relaxed slightly, tipping his head. "Yeah, you're right."

"It's a vacation, after all," I teased. "Can't leave us at home twiddling our thumbs."

He snorted, popping the rest of the bacon into his mouth. He chewed before he said, "We'll go see all the attractions this area has to offer: the creek, the general store, and the gas station."

"Sounds like a thrilling outing."

Once we'd finished our plates and Grace had finally started to eat her own food, Troy got to work cleaning up. He hulked over the kitchen sink, scrubbing at dishes and pans. I could hardly rip my gaze off his broad back and the muscles straining at the fabric of his shirt.

I hadn't been with a man in *years*. Jericho and I formalized our separation over a year ago, but we'd been distant and fractured for so long before then—probably since before I'd even given birth to

Grace. The last year of living with Jericho had been like walking on eggshells. I'd forgotten what it felt like to really *crush* on someone.

After airplaning the last bite of eggs into Grace's mouth, I took the plate over to the sink.

"You're an excellent breakfast cook," I told him. His arm brushed mine as he turned, a smile curling at his lips.

"I'll add that to my resume," he said.

"What does the resume say now? Bodyguard...fitness expert...breakfast specialist..."

He tipped his head. "Don't make me blush. But you forgot chauffer."

I laughed, swatting at his arm. "How could I forget that?"

Troy winked at me as he took the plate and rinsed it off. "Just part of the bodyguard life. Gotta be ready for anything."

"Does Lenny have any coffee in this joint?" I opened random cabinets, looking for the good stuff. "I can brew us a pot."

"I might have seen some over here." He jerked his chin toward a different area of the kitchen. "I didn't even think about coffee."

"You don't drink coffee?" My voice came out practically a screech. "That should go on your resume as well. As a warning."

The genuine smile that covered his face was one I wanted to take a picture of and remember forever.

"I do sometimes. I just try not to get too used to anything."

I knocked his hip with mine as I headed for the other side of the kitchen to continue my hunt. I found a small jar of instant coffee, which was better than nothing.

"This will have to do for now. But we definitely need to get some in town." I filled the tea kettle with water and set it on high on the stove before I leaned against the countertop, my gaze drifting back to Grace as she selected a different crayon from the box. "Where are you heading after this? Back to New York?"

"For just a little bit. And then I'm heading to Ecuador."

"Ecuador." I tried to hide some of my surprise, and the slightest bit of disappointment. Not because I didn't want him to visit a place as fabulous as Ecuador. But because it reminded me that this sweet cocoon was only destined to be a short-lived fantasy. Something like a fever dream, until it went *poof* and the fever broke. "That sounds fun. Is that a vacation or a job?"

"For a job." He snapped the water off, drying his hands as he turned my way. "Something new that came up."

I could already imagine him breezing through open air markets in Ecuador, wearing sunglasses as he smiled into the sun on a coastal beach. "You've got the best job."

"It has its perks."

"I'd say more than perks. What did you tell me during Jordan and Seven's Christmas party? That you'd been to LA, Paris, Miami, and London all within six months last year?"

"That's right." His gaze made that dangerous trek from my face down my body again, as though sizing me up. Deep inside, I hoped it was a precursor to him tossing me over his shoulder. But the faintest whiff of that thought had my logical side swooping in.

Starting something with a bachelor like him is the last thing you should do.

Last year it had been LA, Paris, Miami, and London. This year, it was New York, Kentucky, Ecuador...and where else? The year had barely begun, and he was three pins deep into the world map already. I just needed to enjoy this weird version of a 'getaway' for what it was: a temporary pause on real life. A chance to regroup.

"You're going to have a good time in Ecuador. You'll have to send me a postcard," I told him, trying to close the door on the part of my mind that wanted to believe I might be able to see him beyond this time in the woods. I walked toward Grace, who was finishing her drawing. "Now let's get ready to go for a drive." I tickled her sides, ready to clear my head with a trip to town. She giggled, then pushed her crayons aside.

"This for you!" She held up her sheet of paper, proudly displaying the multi-color scribbles that loosely resembled a snowman.

"Oh, Grace. Are you for real?" Troy took the paper gingerly, looking genuinely touched. "This is incredible. You drew this all yourself?"

Grace nodded shyly, burrowing into my side.

"I'm gonna keep this forever. Thank you." Troy took it to the fridge and stuck it behind a Kentucky-shaped magnet. "We'll keep it here for now so I can see it all the time."

Grace grinned up at me, her eyes twinkling. I could tell they were on their way to becoming best friends.

Once I had a mug of underwhelming instant coffee, I ushered Grace into the bedroom so we could get dressed to go shopping. Once she was in some cute leopard print leggings and her favorite pink sweater, I changed into my own matching mommy outfit: leopard print leggings and a camel colored sweatshirt. I'd always wanted to do the matchy-matchy thing with my daughter and here we were. It was *glorious*.

When we emerged from the bedroom, Troy was shrugging on his dark coat. His eyes widened.

"I don't think I've seen anything cuter in my life," he said.

"There's more where this came from," I warned him. "I've been waiting to match my daughter since before she was born. I think I packed about six matching outfits on top of everything else I brought along."

We shrugged on our coats and headed out into the crisp morning. Our boots crunched over the frosty gravel, breath coming out in comical puffs in front of us. The trip into town held the same edge of wonder that I'd expect on a vacation—everything felt new, exciting, slightly foreign even though we were barely an hour away from my parents' house. Like I was waking up and seeing the world for the first time after so many years of barely absorbing my surroundings.

The store we shopped at was cute but stuffy, a side-of-the-road outpost packed full of the essentials, a meat stand, and a very small vegetable cooler. Grace picked out a banana and another pack of crayons as part of her haul, while Troy and I loaded up on veggies, rotisserie chicken, and coffee. At the counter, Troy blocked my path as I angled to get closer with my wallet out. I couldn't hold in the laughter as he blocked my hands no matter which way I tried to come at the register.

"You're not paying," he informed me.

"You really don't have to foot the bill."

"I don't have to, but I am."

Once we'd checked out, Grace wiggled her fingers at Troy, urging him to pick her up.

Troy blinked down at her. "What's that?"

"She wants you to carry her." I tried to hide my smile. Grace had warmed up to him fast—not just here at the cabin, but during the Christmas party last month as well.

Grace hopped excitedly in front of him. "Toy, pick me up!"

She loved making new friends, but I couldn't help but think she liked how big and strong Troy was too.

Same, girl.

"Oh my God, if that doesn't just melt my heart." He picked her up easily, holding her in his left arm as he scooped up the rest of the bags from the counter with his free hand.

"You need a hand?" I asked him, following behind as we headed for the front doors with the jingle bell on it. He still had a slight limp that I could tell he was trying to hide, the stubborn man. I slipped my phone out of my purse, snapping a quick picture of the scene in front of me. His broad back, Grace's too-cute-to-handle pigtails, all the bags dangling from his right hand.

"I got it," he said, but I darted in front of him to open the back-door to the Jeep.

"You need to let me do *something*," I told him.

"You did plenty," he said, plunking Grace in the booster seat as though she weighed nothing. "You got in my Jeep when I told you to come to the cabin. And you let me pay inside just now."

"That seems like a technicality," I said.

Grace giggled as he fumbled briefly with the seatbelt. "You can do the seatbelt, I guess."

He stepped away, smirking at me, and I caught a puff of his woodsy scent. My eyes fluttered shut—*dear lord.* I wanted to crawl inside his jacket and live there.

I got Grace buckled in and kissed the tip of her nose. Once I'd settled back into the front seat, I had an incoming call. My mother.

My stomach pitched to my feet as I answered.

"Hello?"

"Maddie, sweetie. How are you two doing?" My mom sounded nervous.

"Doing well," I said. "Slept great. Just picked up some stuff to make dinner. What's up?"

"Jericho just came by again."

My eyes slid to the clock in the Jeep. It was barely nine-thirty.

"He demanded to know where you were," my mom went on. "I didn't tell him anything, but..." The tremble in her voice betrayed the emotion there. "He was mad, sweetie."

Troy's attention sizzled on me as I spoke to my mom.

"Was Dad there? Did he say anything when he left?" I asked, my voice sticking to my throat.

"Yes, your father was here, thankfully. Jericho said he hoped you didn't plan on staying gone because he needed to see his daughter."

I pressed my head to the back of the seat, the familiar knot of anxiety cinching tight in my gut. "Thanks for letting me know." Truthfully, I had no idea how long it made sense to stay away. Was forever an option? At some point, I'd have to face him. "If he bothers you again or you get scared, call the police, okay?"

I couldn't believe I was recommending calling the police over my soon-to-be ex-husband. But deep down inside, I wasn't surprised at all.

I'd known since the beginning that Jericho wasn't the one for me...but I'd thought that marriage and starting a family would change him. Help him tame that dark, insidious thread inside him.

And though I'd always done my best to make sure that thread never snapped...it had snapped anyway.

Now, it was time to get to work cleaning up the mess. Claiming a new future for me and my daughter.

CHAPTER SEVEN

TROY

"Do you want me to pour you some more?"

Maddie's simple question and big, hazel eyes were like a spear through my chest. With the fireplace crackling behind her and the entire cabin coated in warmth and ease, I knew the answer to her question.

"I think I've had enough beer." If I took another sip, I'd scoop her into my arms and take her up to the loft. After a full day of exploring town, crunching through the woods around the cabin, and sharing both lunch and dinner with her and Grace, my heart felt fuller than it had in...it was too long to remember.

As a result, I was hanging by a thread around this woman.

"Well I hope you won't judge if I have some more. After all, it's adult time." She stuck her tongue out at me as she filled her glass again. We'd been sharing one big bottle of beer that we found tucked in the back of Len's fridge, something light and locally brewed. Grace had gone down to bed about twenty minutes ago, after a bustling evening of playing a game I'd accidentally invented with her called *Twisty Monkey*. I'd let her dangle from my bicep earlier, made the mistake of spinning, and then Twisty Monkey was born. The girl was obsessed with it. I could almost feel myself still spinning. Maddie and I were now alone at the kitchen island. I told myself this was just a regular adult hangout session.

I needed to convince myself it wouldn't go further.

"Have as much as you want, Maddie."

Her cheeks flushed after I said it, which had me curious.

"Why are you blushing?"

"I'm not."

"You clearly are."

Her cheeks stayed rosy. "It's just hot in here." She twisted to look at the fireplace, then made a display of fanning herself. "See? It's just so warm."

"Take your sweater off then."

Her eyes widened slightly. "Uh...I don't know about that."

It was cute to see her squirm. Maybe she had her mind on the 'adult' side of things like I did. "Should we go outside? I can make a fire."

Her eyes lit up. "Can we?"

I curled my hand into a fist beneath the table, resisting the urge to tug the end of her loose ponytail. Fuck, she was gorgeous. Rosy-cheeked and decked out in leggings; sipping beer and talking about everything with me from world travel to how to sprout an avocado. She was a little brunette snack that I wanted to gobble up.

"We can do anything we want," I told her, wondering if she knew how literally I intended that. My knee groaned as I stood, but I ignored it. "Len's got a firepit and some chairs out back. Let's go."

I wanted to grab her hand and keep her close as we walked outside, but I didn't. Over twenty four hours with this woman and I was losing my head. I wasn't the type of guy to 'play house'—that had never been my goal in life, and it still wasn't.

The only women that graced my beds were the type that didn't stick around for long. That was by design, because that was the only thing that felt right to me. After my chaotic and vagabond upbringing, I kept my distance from the family unit. Stability had never been within reach back then, so I created it the only way I knew how as an adult: staying the fuck away from anything permanent.

Everything about Maddie and Grace screamed *permanent*. Getting involved in that was not a wise choice...but I couldn't help myself, either.

I needed to clear my head, and the cold night air would do the trick.

We shrugged on our coats and boots before slipping out the side door. The firepit sat several yards away from the window of Maddie's bedroom, so we weren't too far from Grace as she slept. Amber exterior lights illuminated the area around the house, allowing me to select the best logs from the woodpile against the house. Maddie hung around the firepit as I stacked the firewood and got the kindling going. I had a fire going within five minutes. She applauded me once the wood was crackling.

"You're such a good fire starter," she cooed, settling onto the wooden bench. I plopped down next to her, admiring my handiwork.

So are you, but a different fire. Also not a thing I would say out loud to this woman.

"I spent a lot of time out in the wild growing up," I told her.

"What, were you raised by wolves?"

I snorted. "Not technically, but it must have seemed like it to those on the outside."

Silence settled between us as the fire grew, consuming the dry wood.

"So your parents were like wolves," she said slowly.

I rubbed my hands together, enjoying the slow build of heat in front of us. But the few inches of space that remained between me and Maddie annoyed me. I wanted them gone. "They were just...trying their best, I guess?" I laughed, but it came out bitter.

Because that's how I still felt about the whole situation. "My dad had some mental health issues that he chose not to take care of. So it meant that me and my mom and my little sister were constantly dealing with the consequences."

Her frown shone brightly in the shifting light of the fire. "That must have been so hard."

"We traveled the US like vagabonds. Or maybe like someone in the witness protection program, I don't know. We lived in a shitty RV and never stayed anywhere for longer than a week."

My voice gave out, though there was so much more I could have said. Those details alone sounded embarrassing enough. I'd spent my entire adolescence trying to hide the evidence of how broken my family life was. Living in the shadow of my father's mental illness made it hard to keep friends, much less attend school. My mother cycled us in and out of public schools, depending on how long we'd stay in the same area. When we weren't in school, she home schooled us. It had been a shit show with a capital Shit.

Maddie reached for my hand, crossing her legs and facing me on the bench. "Seriously?"

"It's okay." I couldn't move my hand away from hers, even though I knew I should. "Ancient history now."

Her frown deepened, and I could tell she wasn't satisfied by my response. "It sounds difficult."

"Well, upside is I got to see a lot of the country. From sea to shining sea."

"That's...definitely unique," she said with a laugh.

"When kids were looking at the Grand Canyon in their textbooks, we were there in the flesh, making breakfast sausage over an open flame after staying illegally overnight in the state park," I went on.

She grinned, but it faded quickly. "Is your father okay now?"

My stomach sank like a rock to my feet and I pulled my hand away from hers. "No. He's worse than ever. I haven't heard from my parents in months and I don't know how to find them. I just gotta wait until he snaps out of it and reaches out. Sometimes my little sister will hear from them and let me know but other than that..."

I swallowed a knot in my throat. It had taken me a long time to realize that my upbringing wasn't normal, much less healthy. It had taken me even longer to realize that all that fear and suspicion I'd absorbed from my father wasn't mine to carry either. Made sense why I'd gravitated toward the military as soon as I was able. Having structure and rules felt like a relief after living in the opposite for so long, while the movement and constantly changing scenery was what I was used to.

"Maybe you could put an airtag on their RV..."

"He'd sniff that out immediately." I rubbed at my face, unsure how deep I wanted to get into my father's mental health concerns...and whether it might change her opinion about *me*. "He's pretty paranoid, worried that the government is tracking him and shit. If he found out I actually was tracking him, it would just confirm all his delusions."

Silence settled between us, broken only by the crackling fire.

"I don't usually talk about my parents with anyone," I admitted after a few moments.

She scooted closer to me, legs crossed as she faced me. "I don't usually escape to a safe house with anyone, either."

My gaze drifted back to her pretty face. Her cheeks were rosy from the cold, and the way she looked at me had me rethinking my need to keep space between us. After all, she'd kissed me—that elephant in the room had to mean something, right? We hadn't brought it up, but maybe we needed to talk about it.

"You picked the right guy to escape with," I told her. "You don't have to worry about any funny business. You can even kiss me again if you need to and I won't make a big deal about it."

Her eyes flashed, reminding me of just how strange this predicament was. I'd connected with her harder and faster than almost anyone in my entire life. But the bodyguard-client rules were ones I believed in and obeyed. Yet she wasn't technically my client...and I wasn't doing anything more than just getting her out of a stressful situation temporarily.

The lines were blurry. I wanted to erase them altogether.

"I might need to again." The teasing tone in her voice was more than clear. A smile curled at her lips.

"Do whatever you need to, Maddie."

She bit her bottom lip, her knee knocking the side of my leg. "Is that thing you said in the restaurant true?"

I propped my arm up on the back of the bench, trying to think back on all the things I'd said there. "Help me out. Which thing? I said a lot of them."

Her cheeks flushed, but not from the cold. She yanked her gaze to the fire and watched it while she spoke. "That you'd been wanting that kiss to happen since New York."

I rubbed at my face again. I'd admitted that in a kiss-drunk moment of honesty. But now, I wasn't sure which way to play it. That was before I'd taken her away to a cabin in the middle of nowhere.

"I probably shouldn't admit that, but yeah. It was true."

She snapped her gaze back to me. "Why shouldn't you admit it?"

I tipped my head, pinning her with a look. "I'm supposed to be helping you, not making out with you."

Her hazel eyes danced in the light of the fire. "What would you do if I kissed you again?"

"Why don't you try it and find out?"

She held my gaze, almost as if waiting to see that I was serious. Then she lifted her chin, looking back toward the fire. "I don't know. I've already kissed you first. Kissing you first the second time would just look desperate."

She had a point. One that my internal gentleman couldn't resist addressing.

I hooked my arm around her waist and brought her against me in a swift, fluid motion. She inhaled sharply, looking up at me with question marks in her eyes.

"Let me make it easier." My voice came out low, hoarse. She was mere inches away now. Her hazel eyes drank me in and the weight of her in my arm, pressed against my body, felt too natural. Like she could stay there forever and I wouldn't even mind. "I'm acutely aware that this is not the time or the place to be coming onto you. But you should know that not a single day has gone by since we met at Seven's party where I didn't think about you or wonder what it would be like to kiss you. And when you showed me the other day at the restaurant, it's all I've wanted since."

Her breath caught, and for a moment, time shuddered to a stop around us. Nothing existed except the endless hazel paradise of her eyes, the amber tang of her perfume, and the crackling fire that had nothing on the energy pounding between us.

I'd laid my cards on the table.

And fuck, I couldn't play the chivalrous part any longer.

I tightened my grip around her and pulled her into me, our lips meeting in a warm, hungry kiss. The scent of her enveloped me, sending me deeper into desire. I traced the contour of her waist through her coat, fingers twitching with the urge to find the hot silk of her skin beneath. Maddie whimpered, fisting the front of my coat as our tongues met. Without even deciding, I hauled her onto my lap, her legs opening up to straddle my waist.

Her thighs tensed around me, locking me in, as our kisses went from tentative to deep and delicious. I traced the edge of her lip with my tongue, coaxing more from her. She hooked her arms around my neck, pressing her curvy frame against my chest. I hated that we had these coats on; I would have done anything to feel the softness of her against my body, to finally get handfuls of her tits like I'd been imagining for weeks.

She pulled back suddenly, resting her forehead against mine.

"I didn't think there was any way you felt the same," she whispered, her gaze darting back and forth across my face.

I grunted, shifting slightly beneath her. My cock had gone from semi to fully hard and the weight of her on top of me had me dizzy from desire.

"From the second I laid eyes on you, Maddie." I kissed the tip of her rosy nose, followed by her cheeks, then along her jawline.

She laughed softly. "We connected pretty hard, didn't we?"

"Like nothing I've felt before." The words tumbled out of my mouth before I had a chance to filter them. But maybe it was okay to say them. "I was so close to begging you to stay in New York, but I knew...it just wouldn't have been an option for you."

Her gaze dropped to the space between us, and I could feel something inside her shift. She nibbled on her bottom lip as I nibbled on her earlobe.

"Yeah," she finally said.

When I tried to kiss her on the lips again, she pressed softly on my chest. There was sadness in her gaze, and something else I didn't fully understand.

"I think I should just go inside," she whispered.

"Why?" I nuzzled her neck, trying to remind her of what we were on the precipice of exploring.

"I don't want to do something I'll regret." She gnawed on the inside of her lip, avoiding my gaze. She slid off my lap, a whoosh of cold air replacing her.

Maybe she didn't mean for the words to be a spear. But they landed like one anyway.

"All right. Goodnight, Maddie." I reached for her hand as she stood from the bench but missed her by an inch. I listened to her steps toward the house; the door creaked open; and then a moment later, it was just me and my thoughts in front of the crackling fire.

There were a thousand reasons why Maddie's decision to pump the brakes was a smart one.

So why couldn't I fully convince myself of it?

CHAPTER EIGHT
MADDIE

"Twisty Monkey! Twisty Monkey!"

Grace's excited pleas for *Twisty Monkey* had been ping-pong-ing off the walls since she woke up. I managed to stave her off long enough to get dressed, brush teeth, and do our hair before she barreled out of the bedroom, looking for Troy.

Excited giggles moments later told me she found him.

I followed behind her tentatively, still feeling some of the awkwardness from the way I'd left things last night.

Pulling myself off a hulking, hard-bodied bodyguard snack like Troy wasn't easy. But I needed to think long-term. Big picture. Even if it meant saying *no* to the one man I fantasized about.

"Look who it is!"

I came into the kitchen to find Troy already doing the spin-and-bicep-curl move that Grace was obsessed with. They were both grinning like crazy, his husky laugh and her shrieking giggles filling the warm cabin. Through the big bay windows at the front of the cabin, fresh snow sparkled on the bare tree limbs and all across the yard.

"Good morning," I called over the fray. I went to go make a pot of coffee with our newfound coffee grounds but I found the coffeepot already full. An empty mug sat beside the coffeemaker with a spoon inside, along with a jar of sugar and some creamer set out.

My eyes watered as I beheld the careful preparation. When I turned to look at Troy, he was spinning underneath the buckhorn chandelier, practically guffawing with laughter as he spun Grace around and around.

This man is perfect. The thought hung uncomfortably inside me as I poured myself a mug of coffee, added sugar, and topped it off with a few drops of creamer. Perfection. It was still early, so I figured I'd return the favor by getting breakfast started while they played. To the chorus of happy shrieks, I whipped together my and Grace's favorite breakfast: my mom's French Toast recipe.

"Okay, Gracie, Troy needs a break." Troy sighed heavily and plopped onto the couch in the great room. Grace curled up next to him on the couch, grinning over at me with ruddy cheeks.

"Mommy did you see?"

"Oh, I saw!" I smiled brightly at her as I beat the eggs in a small bowl. "You have so much fun with Troy, don't you?"

"I wub Toy."

That was her way of saying 'love'. It made my heart break—I figured they'd become fast friends, but now she loved him on day three. This was just going to make things harder when it came time for Troy to go to Ecuador and for us to resume our regular lives.

My stomach twisted. What would my regular life look like now? Constantly thinking about this handsome, thoughtful, protective man while he gallivanted the world? I fought to ignore that train of thought.

After taking a rest on the couch, Troy finally joined me in the kitchen, his limp still noticeable only if I stared long enough. He brushed past me, peering over my shoulder at what I was doing. Electricity sparked beneath my skin.

"You get your coffee?" His voice was a low rumble. My thighs tensed, wanting to pick up right where we'd left off last night. The solid heat of him between my legs was a memory that wouldn't let me fall asleep last night.

"I did. Thank you. Did you sleep well?"

"Fine and dandy." I heard mugs clinking behind me as I continued prepping. A moment later, he was at my side, pouring more coffee in my mug. "You need to be topped off."

I set down the spoon and bowl, lifting my mug to clink against his. "Thanks for the coffee. You made it perfectly. Which leads me to wonder: do you have any flaws?"

He tipped his head in thought as he leaned against the countertop beside me. "I don't think I do."

"And so humble too."

He winked at me over his steaming mug of coffee before he took a sip. "All right, fine, maybe I have a few flaws. But I won't admit them because if I ignore them they don't exist, right?"

"I think that's how that works."

We shared a laugh, but it faded once Troy's phone started ringing. He fished it out of the pocket of his gray sweatpants, frowning at the screen. "I should take this."

"Do what you need to do. I'm going to make us French toast."

He answered the phone call and drifted toward the other side of the cabin, where I could see him and only sort of hear him. I tried not to act too interested in his call, even though I was dying to know who it was and what they wanted. Everything about Troy interested me.

I checked on Grace once the toast was ready to pop onto the warmed griddle, and found her happily coloring in her coloring book in the great room. I returned to the kitchen, ready to start cooking the egg-slathered toast, but couldn't prevent myself from tuning into Troy's conversation.

"Mm-hmm…a few weeks there sounds good…though I haven't taken Spanish lessons in a long time."

I focused on the pop-sizzle of the toast.

"Right…" Troy went on, only bits and pieces of his conversation making it over to me. "…but it's best to be prepared with rum." His rich chuckle filled the cabin a moment later.

Once the French toast was golden, I piled them on a plate and called Grace over. She dropped the crayons and bolted into the kitchen just as Troy wrapped up his phone call.

"Toy! Time to eat!" she called in her sing-song voice.

"This looks awesome." Troy ruffled her hair as he eased onto one of the stools at the island. He helped her pop up onto her own stool and she beamed at him, her blonde topknot already slightly askew from the endless rounds of Twisty Monkey.

"My favorite," she stated proudly, reaching for her fork. "My mommy's favorite too."

"Your mommy's a good cook, huh?" Troy winked at me as he cut into the French toast. After a big bite, he nodded and groaned. "Wow. What's the secret ingredient, Maddie?" He tucked into more, and I could tell he wasn't just feeding me a line. "This is so dang good."

"I can't spill my chef secrets," I teased, enjoying the view I had of him inhaling my family recipe. He finished the plate in record time. "You must have worked out extra hard this morning. Hungry boy."

"Hungry is an understatement." He met my gaze, something challenging there. Better not to dive into that. I wanted to move to lighter conversation but couldn't think past what I'd overheard him say on his phone call.

"So who were you talking to before? Sounded interesting." I focused on my food so that maybe he wouldn't be able to read any accidental emotions that might come through on my face.

"That was my newest employer. His name is Nash Nightingale, he called to square away some details for my first assignment. He and his twin brother run a massive real estate empire that's only been growing over the past few years."

"Is that why they're taking you to Ecuador? To expand business or something?"

"It sounds like it, but to be honest with you, I have no idea." Troy took a sip of his coffee. "Not my job to ask. I just need to be where they tell me."

"You're a good man to have around." I finally dared to meet his gaze. His warm brown eyes pierced my heart. "Let me know if you ever need a recommendation, I'll leave you a good Yelp review."

He cracked a grin. "That's sweet of you."

Pleasant silence settled between us as I helped Grace cut some pieces of her toast and get them into her mouth. "So how long will you be gone?" This time, I made sure not to look his way at all, because I knew he'd see the real question behind my words: *will I ever see you again?*

"I don't have a return ticket," he said slowly, then took a sip of his coffee. "So, I guess that means—I have no idea."

The corners of my mouth trembled as I struggled to keep an easygoing look on my face. I did not want him to see how crestfallen I felt on the inside. I didn't even want to admit to myself how crestfallen I truly was. It just didn't seem right to want a man so deeply, especially in these circumstances. No, it just sounded *crazy*.

"Send me a postcard, okay?" I ventured a small smile. "I can show the kids at school, they'd think that was so cool."

"Maybe I can come by with some stuff for Ecuador for a show-and-tell."

"That would be cute." The idea was genuinely touching. "But Louisville is so far out of your way. What a silly detour to make."

"Not a silly detour if I get to see you."

His words thudded between us, causing me to jerk my gaze up to meet his. His eyes looked hungry again. I took a quick bite of food, eager to distract myself with something. *Anything.*

"Besides, I need to see how Miss Maddie keeps her classroom," Troy went on. He grinned down at Grace, ruffling her hair. "Have you seen your mommy's classroom? Does she keep it as cute as she is?"

I couldn't fight the grin.

"I bet you decorate for all the holidays."

"You make it sound like an accusation," I teased.

"It sort of is."

"Well, you're right." I scrunched up my face at him. "I'm legally required to decorate for every holiday as an elementary teacher."

He watched me with an easy grin, the kind that made it impossible not to sit there and drink him in.

"Toy, can we play outside today?" Grace's innocent question cut through the desire building in the air between me and Troy.

Troy ripped his gaze off me, looking down at Grace. He pretended to think about it, then he said, "Yeah. I don't think there's anything I'd rather do."

Once we were all finished with breakfast, Troy offered to clean up but I waved him off. "You have important things to do. Like playing outside and possibly a few bonus rounds of Twisty Monkey."

"Shh." He glanced back at Grace to see if she'd overheard. "That game makes me dizzy."

"Three-year-olds only want to do the dizziest, most puke-inducing thing possible," I informed him. "You're gonna have to buck up. Surely your bodyguard training prepared you for this."

"Nothing at boot camp prepared me for Twisty Monkey," he said with a severe look.

Grace gasped loudly. "Did you say Twisty Monkey?"

Troy groaned softly, but when he turned to Grace, he had the biggest grin. "I absolutely did."

The rest of the morning disappeared like that: warm, homey, sun-dappled moments that burrowed straight into my long-term memories. For lunch, Troy made lunch meat sandwiches that provided yet another chance for him and Grace to connect. And after lunch, they finally got suited up to head outside.

"You coming with?" Troy asked.

"I think I'm going to curl up by the fireplace and read." I bit my bottom lip, almost embarrassed to admit it. I knew how much of an introverted homebody I was, which was why fall and winter were my favorite months of the year. Not that I didn't love spring and summer for their own strengths, but I was a supreme fan of coziness, books, and everything seasonally appropriate. Add in a totally unnecessary throw blanket and I was a happy woman.

Troy looked like he was fighting a smile as he nodded. "Yeah. That's exactly what a cute ass elementary teacher would say."

I scrunched up my face. "You said the A-word."

Troy looked down at Grace but she didn't seem to notice. "Okay, got a free pass on that one. Let's go outside, Gracie-bell!"

He had a nickname for her now. Be still my heart. I watched them through the window as they stepped tentatively into the snow. Troy had her hand in his as they ventured into the side yard, right near the firepit where I'd straddled the steel of Troy's legs just last night. My eyes fluttered shut as the memories returned. Was there really such a problem with just getting one taste of him?

I sank onto the couch nearest the fireplace, determined to forget about all things Troy. Once I'd found my place in my paperback, I quickly got lost in reading. Time melted away in a blissful state. I wasn't sure how much time had passed when I heard the muffled sounds of crying.

My skin prickled and I sat up. That had to be Grace—unless I was imagining it. I set down the book and hurried to find my boots and coat. As soon as I opened the side door a moment later, the crying grew louder.

Outside, Grace sat in an Adirondack chair at the firepit. Troy knelt in front of her, cradling her ankle in his big hand as he inspected her leg. I hurried over to them, kneeling down to eye-level with Grace.

"Are you okay honey?" I asked her. Looking at Troy, I said, "What happened?"

She drew a ragged breath, her eyes rimmed with redness.

"We were playing hide and seek," he said. "She hid by the wood pile and hurt her leg."

I stroked Grace's head and she looked up at me. "I got a boo boo."

"Do you think your leg is okay?" I asked her.

She nodded emphatically, but Troy looked concerned. He gingerly tested bending her knee followed by extending it.

"Nothing hurts, right?" he asked her.

"I think she was just scared," I said softly. The way she'd been crying, paired with her lack of reaction as Troy inspected her, told me that. I could identify Grace's cries in a line-up at this point. Each one meant a slightly different thing.

"Those logs tried to get you, didn't they?" Troy asked, coming to standing. He helped her to her feet, and within a few moments, she was beaming up at both of us, wisps of her blonde hair escaping her knit cap.

"Mommy, can we take Toy home with us?"

The question knocked the wind out of me. I had no idea how to answer that. My gaze snapped up to find Troy's, and he had a mischievous grin waiting for me.

"I, uh...well, Troy has things he needs to do after we're done at the cabin," I started to explain. Sometimes, I was glad my daughter was three. She didn't have any idea how bad I was fumbling over the question.

But Troy, on the other hand, could see and understand it all.

When her face started to fall, I hurried to add, "I'm sure he'll come visit someday."

Grace's brows furrowed together as she wiped a hair from her face. "But Toy will be good, right Toy?"

His brows shot up and he nodded, the start of a smirk on his lips. "Oh yes. I'll be good." He stepped closer, adding in a low voice for only me to hear, "Unless you don't want me to be."

Heat shuddered through me. He held my gaze, his arm brushing against mine as he followed Grace toward the house. A waft of his cedar cologne reached me, and I almost needed the sturdiness of his arm to ensure my knees didn't buckle.

Between his thoughtfulness, the safety he provided, and his level ten handsomeness...I was a goner. The man slept thirty feet from my room and each night that I went to bed without more of those hot kisses seemed like a wasted opportunity.

Maybe that needed to change.

The longer we whiled away our days at the cabin, the harder it was to remember why getting a taste of Troy was a bad idea.

CHAPTER NINE

TROY

THE FIRST THING I became aware of the next morning was the soft chiming of my alarm. Seven a.m. wakeup call, every day, without fail. Even in the middle of nowhere Kentucky while in this weird transition between gigs.

I launched an arm to the nightstand to silence it, staring up at the wooden peak of the cabin above the loft. And that's when I became aware of the next thing about my day: the fact that Maddie still hadn't graced this bed once.

And that was a damn shame.

I heaved a sigh, rolling onto my side like this might somehow shake the thoughts loose so they could spill out of my head. But no. There was no losing these thoughts about Maddie. Just one look at her soft, curvy body, her long brunette ponytail and the way she filled out her leggings and tops could get me hard.

And now I was hard just thinking about her. *You're like a goddamn teenager around this woman.*

I couldn't remember the last time I met a woman who could turn me on with every glance or sigh. But that was Maddie – a perfect ten. An amazing mother, a sweet schoolteacher, and a woman who just clicked with me. At almost thirty-five years old, I knew how rare that was.

In my life, I usually tried to avoid any chance for the click with women. It was easier that way. Better to just have a night or two of fun, and then go our separate ways.

But the problem with Maddie was that I didn't *want* to separate from her.

And that was...a little uncomfortable for me.

I tossed back the covers, sitting up with a deep sigh. Time to start the day.

I chugged the glass of water I left on the nightstand, hurried into the bathroom to take a piss and brush my teeth, then I pulled on some workout shorts to get started on the routine. Pushups, sit-ups, squats, and crunches—until I sweat my ass off. That was the nonnegotiable way to start the day, and the only way to keep my head straight. By the time I was done, sunlight streamed in through the floor to ceiling windows on the north end of the house, showcasing the frosty branches and sparkling snowfall outside. As I wiped my face with a towel, I heard rustling from downstairs.

Followed by the soft pitter-patter of feet.

Soft thumps up the stairs.

And then finally, two big eyes peering around the banister of the loft staircase.

"*Gracie.*" Maddie's urgent hiss ricocheted through the cabin. "Get back here."

Grace didn't make a move, just continued spying on me as though I couldn't see her. I sank onto the edge of the bed and waved.

"Hey there, cutie. Should you be up here?"

Footsteps sounded on the staircase again—this time Maddie's. She appeared behind Grace a moment later, her eyes turning into saucers as she spotted me.

"Oh my God. I'm so sorry Troy."

"It's no problem." I had to fight a smile as I watched Maddie's cheeks flush. Sure, I was shirtless and sweating, but it wasn't like they'd caught me doing something bad. Maybe she liked what she saw.

"There was no keeping her in the bedroom," Maddie went on, smoothing Grace's hair, "she just had to come say good morning."

"Good morning," I told the little blondie pipsqueak. She smiled shyly.

"Sorry to interrupt," Maddie waved her fingers in my direction, "whatever you were doing here."

While she spoke, I drank in her just-woke-up perfection. The messy topknot, the olive green cotton pajama shorts and loose t-shirt that allowed me a tantalizing glimpse of the peaks of her breasts. I closed my fists, dying to pull her into the bed and see what happened.

"Just trying to tone up a little," I said, wiping at the side of my face with the sweat towel. "I hear schoolteachers like it when guys are fit so I'm just doing whatever I can."

She pursed her lips, something mischievous coming over her face. "They certainly don't mind it. We should get back downstairs though. Come on, Grace. Let's go find your coloring books."

Grace pouted as she started down the stairs.

"But Maddie, *you* should stay." I knew it was impossible to do what I wanted while Grace was awake for the day. But I couldn't keep the words from tumbling out of my mouth.

She dipped her chin, sending me an admonishing look. But I saw the desire flash across her face as well.

She wanted it, even if she didn't want to act on it.

"Maybe you can just come give me good morning hug?" I suggested. My heartbeat pounded through my veins, pushing me to bold lengths. She'd already pumped the brakes once, and I respected that.

But with her looking like the woman of my dreams, just a pair of thin cotton shorts hiding what I wanted to get to know, there was no holding back.

She looked down the stairs, then nodded. "Grace went down," she said, and then darted across the loft. I held out my hands and she filled the space there, hooking her arms around my neck with a giggle.

And just like that, we picked up where we'd left off at the firepit the other night.

"Good morning," I murmured into her collarbone. My eyes fluttered shut as I tried to remember every single sensation from this hug: the softness of her body pressed against me, the way her tits smashed against my chest, the light and feminine amber perfume that still clung to her. "Remind me why you aren't sleeping up here with me each night?"

She laughed, but it sounded wispy. "Troy, we both know that's a bad idea."

"Do we?" I couldn't keep myself from dragging my lips across the exposed skin of her shoulder. Her oversized t-shirt was in danger of being torn off.

She shifted against me, allowing her hips to splay open and straddle me again. I grunted as her thick thighs settled on either side of my body.

"Pretty sure you sleeping in my bed is the best idea in the world," I said, nipping at her earlobe.

She shivered in my arms. "I'm not disagreeing with you."

I smoothed my hands over the small of her back, down over the mounds of her ass. She arched into me, and I locked my arms tight around her so that no space remained between us.

"If you come try to give me a hug later tonight, I'll make sure you don't go back down those stairs."

She giggled, and then pressed her lips against mine for a deep, hungry kiss. I caught the taste of peppermint on her tongue, and we kissed so passionately that I almost missed the small voice say, "Mommy?"

Maddie was off of me in a flash, turning to greet Grace at the top of the stairs.

"Hey, honey!" She sounded too friendly, almost maniacal. "What's wrong? Did I take too long to come down?"

Grace blinked a few times, looking between the two of us.

"Does Toy have a boo boo?" she asked.

"Umm," Maddie started.

"Is that why you kissing him?" she finished.

Maddie cleared her throat, nodding. "Yes. He hurt his...face."

Grace blinked, and then bounded back down the stairs. Maddie pressed a hand to her forehead, sending me a pointed look.

"You are...too much. I can't control myself around you."

"That makes two of us," I informed her.

She sighed, heading for the staircase. "I need to go get dressed."

"I think you should stay exactly like you are. I love these jammies."

When she looked over at me, I could see the genuine smile fighting to take over. "They're literally from the clearance rack at a thrift store."

"You could wear a potato sack and I'd be into it."

She laughed, shaking her head. "You either don't meet a lot of women or..."

"I promise you. I meet plenty. And I don't want to see any of them in a potato sack."

Her throat bobbed and then she drew a deep breath, looking away. "I need to go downstairs."

I didn't protest this time, but I did watch every step she took going downstairs. I was fully hard from the two minutes she spent in my lap, and I had every intention of showing her a great time in the loft that night.

After a quick shower, I joined them downstairs in the kitchen. This time, Maddie had prepared the coffee for *me*. She wore leggings and an oversized sweatshirt today. I slyly squeezed an ass cheek on my way past, out of Grace's line of vision.

"Extra good morning to you." I poured myself some coffee and she came to my side, knocking my hip.

"Yeah I'd say it got off on the right foot." She grinned but it faded quickly, something clouding her gaze. "I hate to kill the vibe, but...my long weekend is coming to an end."

It was Monday, day four of our getaway.

"I've got some admin work to catch up on today but...I have to be at work tomorrow." Maddie crossed her arms, gnawing on the inside of her cheek as she looked out at the cabin. Today was an admin day for her building so no students were reporting for class.

"Do you want to go back to your parents' house?" I blew on the steaming coffee, leaning against the countertop to face her.

She shrugged. "That's fine. I have to go back there eventually." She seemed like she was going to add more but thought better of it.

"Or..." I prompted her.

She laughed, shaking her head. "Or nothing. I was going to say we could find some way for you to smuggle us to Ecuador with you, but I don't think that's a great way for a three-year-old to travel."

I could read behind the words. She wanted more time with me. Just like I wanted more time with her. "What if we just stay here until I have to head north to catch the flight?"

"But I can't skip tomorrow—"

"I'll drive you in," I told her. "It's a longer commute than normal, but it can be done."

She tilted her head. "Once you drop me and Grace off at school...what would you even do all day? That's such a long time to just mill around, waiting for us."

"I'll figure it out. Besides, someone needs to take care of your car now that the tires are repaired. Let me handle that." I sipped at my coffee, holding her pretty hazel gaze as long as she'd let me. "I'm not letting you out of my sight as long as I can help it. Unless you tell me to fuck off, in which case...I'd think about it."

Her shoulders shook with laughter. I reached over and poked her in the belly. "So what do you say?"

"I'm afraid to admit to you how much I'd like to continue our cabin staycation," she finally said.

"That sounds like a yes."

"It's a 'yes, but I can't believe you actually want to drive in and out of Louisville every day to make this work'."

She had no idea the things I was ready to do for her. Scaring off her ex, hiding her away, and being her personal chauffeur were just the beginning...and that surprised even me.

Our Monday at the cabin disappeared amid homecooked meals, a surprise batch of cookies, and a holiday movie marathon even though Christmas was behind us. Lenny probably couldn't imagine what a home his cabin had turned into. I took a picture of us beneath the buckhorn chandelier—he liked daily updates of his work of art—and sent it to him with the caption: *Still haven't burned the place down. Thought you'd be happy to know.*

I don't think he realized just how much sexual tension his cabin contained either. Maddie and I specialized in lingering looks and heated touches. While Grace was awake, I was committed to not having another slip like what had happened in the morning. But the longer that Maddie was breathing and within view, the harder it became to keep my fingers and lips from wandering her way.

Around seven-thirty, Maddie clapped her hands together. "Okay Grace! Time for a bath, we're late getting to bed."

The poor thing had no idea that her mom was actually *early* in getting her to bed, by at least a full half hour. I gave Grace a good-night hug, per her request, before she shuffled off to the bathroom to do her nighttime routine with her mom. While they were busy, I caught up with Seven via text message.

SEVEN: Everything okay over there? Haven't heard much from either of you.

TROJAN: Peachy keen.

SEVEN: Oh my god, you two are boning already, aren't you?

I was *so glad* there were a thousand miles between Seven and I right now, because I would have punched the fuck out of his shoulder for his annoyingly correct observation.

TROJAN: Not sure what I said that suggested that, but okay.

SEVEN: You have never once used the phrase 'peachy keen' in your life. You're either boning the ward or you've been abducted and this is your cry for help.

That fucker. He knew me too well. But I wouldn't let him win so easily.

TROJAN: Abducted. Send help.

Seven called me seconds later. I answered with a laugh. "I'm glad you're so quick to react when you think I've been abducted."

"So you haven't been abducted, which means you *are* boning the ward."

My gaze slid to the hallway. I could hear the muffled undertones of the shower running in the bathroom. "Can neither confirm nor deny."

"You know," Seven started, sounding fucking smug, "a wise man once told me to never get with a client—"

"Maddie's not a client," I reminded him.

"Why don't you just *go find someone else and get it out of your system*?" Seven's smug smile could be tasted as he said my own words back to me. And I hated it. "That same wise man told me that."

"This wise man sounds like a very handsome, smart, and capable person who was speaking to you from a very specific point in his life."

Seven's laughter boomed through the phone. "You are so busted."

"And you are annoying. I need to go."

"Everything good over there?"

"Yeah. About to be a lot better once you let me get back to what I was doing." As I hung up, I heard Seven's laughter booming through the phone. My cheeks hurt from how hard I grinned. I loved that dude. He was the closest thing I had to a brother. We'd been thick as thieves since day one at boot camp, and I was happy to report that our friendship was even stronger over fifteen years later.

Ever since he'd gotten serious with Jordan—the one I'd told him to stay away from because not only was she his client, she was the little sister of his employer at the time—he'd been putting the pressure on me to settle down too.

Well I had no intentions of settling down. At least not like he had.

But part of me wondered if there wasn't some happy medium to be found.

I checked emails while Maddie and Grace moved from the bathroom to the bedroom. I heard some muffled giggles, followed by a long stretch of silence. Just when I thought maybe Maddie had fallen asleep in there, the bedroom door creaked open.

Maddie slipped out, hurrying toward me. I straightened from where I'd been leaning against the kitchen counter as she launched herself at me. I barely had time to catch her, laughter cascading out of me as she clung to me like a little panda.

"You really missed me, huh?"

I hoisted her in my arms until her thighs settled on either side of me. She was at eye level now, and grinning at me with mischief written across her face.

"I was hoping we could pick up where we left off this morning." Her arms slid around my neck, wrists locking behind my head. I squeezed the thickness of her upper thighs, a low rumble of appreciation escaping me. She could stay here forever as far as I was concerned. Nothing felt better than the weight of her in my arms.

In lieu of more words, I leaned forward and finished the kiss I'd been thinking about since eight a.m. Our lips met hungrily, and she kissed me like she'd been thinking about the same thing nonstop too. I pressed my tongue past her lips, consuming the taste of her, getting drunk on this passion pulsing between us. A soft whimper escaped her as she tightened her thighs around me, erasing every last inch of space between us.

I kissed her like I'd been wandering a maze for years and she was the exit. Something deep inside me sighed with relief. Something I wasn't quite ready to explore, much less understand.

Our kisses grew more desperate. Maddie rocked her hips against me, which sent my pulse pounding. I'd been fully hard since the second she stepped out of the bedroom and I only wanted more of this woman.

"Oh my God." Maddie rested her forehead against mine, drawing deep breaths of air. "These kisses are making me dizzy."

I nuzzled the side of her neck, needing more of her sweet scent. "Me too. You're a really good kisser."

She bit at her bottom lip, her eyes drifting shut. "So are you."

"I'm good at other things too." I set her on the kitchen island. "You're about to find out."

She giggled, wriggling her hips. "And on the countertop?"

"No better place." I tugged at the hem of her sweatshirt, pulling it over her head. Once it was tossed aside, I eyed the plain white tee she had on underneath. Cute, but it ultimately had to go. I pushed my hands beneath the cotton, searching out the warm curves beneath. She shivered, her thighs squeezing around my hips.

"You look so fucking cute in everything you wear," I told her, running my hands over the swell of her hips, her belly, up over her rib cage, "but I think you'd look absolutely stunning wearing nothing at all."

Pink stained her cheeks. "It's nothing to get worked up about."

"Excuse me?" I took a step back, sweeping my gaze from top to toes. "Are we talking about the same sexy ass mama right now? Because I am worked up."

She laughed, and I dipped in for another kiss.

"Don't be shy," I told her, whispering into her ear. "You're the sexiest woman I've laid on eyes on, and I can prove it." I reached for her hand, guiding it in between our bodies. Her palm ran over the thick ridge of my cock, covered by my jeans. "See what you do to me?"

A shiver ran through her. The shyness in her gaze was replaced with heat.

"And that's *with* your clothes on," I reminded her.

She bit at her bottom lip, moving her palm up and down the length of my hard-on. I grunted, flexing my hips. "Mmm. That's all from me?"

"All from you." I tugged at her earlobe with my teeth. "I've been imagining the things I wanted to do to you since last month. And now I get my chance."

She cupped the sides of my face, capturing my lips in a sweet kiss. When we broke apart, she said, "I really didn't think you felt the same way."

"You really must never look in a mirror. You have no idea how sexy you are."

"No, I mean..." Her throat bobbed. "With Grace and all. I figured you'd see a single mom and run the other way."

It almost didn't compute. I tried to see the meaning behind her words. "Do you think I'd run because you have a daughter... or because..."

Her cheeks flushed again and her gaze dropped to my chest. She smoothed her hand over my t-shirt. "Not just because I'm a mom, but...things change after you have a baby. Everyone knows that. I breastfed. I carried a human inside me. I'm not a perfect ten, Troy."

"Hm." I gripped her by the hips, tugging her flush against me. The pieces were clicking into place. And the picture the puzzle created was that her ex-douchebag likely made her feel like shit a lot. "I guess it's time for the exam then."

"The exam?" Laughter leaked out the edges of her words.

"Yeah. I'll accept nothing less than a perfect ten. It's my right as a blue-blooded male." We shared an amused look from my thick-ass sarcasm. I tugged off her shirt, revealing a taupe, lacy bra, covering the most perfect set of breasts I could remember seeing. I smoothed my hands over her belly rolls, taking big handfuls of the overspill from the waistband of her leggings. I grunted, then pushed my hands up, underneath her bra. Perfect handfuls. I swiped a thumb over her taut nipples as my free hand reached behind her to unclasp the bra.

Her breathing came out a little quicker and her head lolled to one side.

"I'd tell you the results of the exam," I said, dragging my lips against her exposed collarbone, "but the truth is no one else's opinion even matters. So whoever made you feel like shit deserves to get my fist into the side of his skull. Tell me who I need to go visit."

"You already met him," she whispered, her chest rising and falling rapidly.

"Noted. I'll add that to my list of grievances for when I run into him next."

A pretty smiled covered her face as I held her tits and kissed the tops of each one in turn.

"And by the way?" *Kiss.* "You're a perfect ten."

"I need to have you around as my personal hype man," she breathed.

"Just wait until I get inside you," I promised before covering her lips with my own.

Because I already knew the truth.

I was a goner for this woman.

CHAPTER TEN

MADDIE

I didn't feel particularly good about having my bare ass cheeks on the kitchen island where we'd had breakfast earlier that morning.

But luckily I knew where the cleaning spray was, and I'd be spraying like crazy later. Because there was no way in hell I was going to interrupt anything that Troy wanted to do right now.

He'd gotten me down to absolutely nothing. I was buck naked and ass spread on the kitchen island. Every inch of my skin was electric and alive as his appreciative gaze swept over me. He wet his bottom lip, shaking his head like he was admiring a piece of art.

"You are going to be such a good nighttime snack," he finally said.

"Do you plan on having a nibble somewhere?" I asked jokingly.

His hot palm slid up my thigh, then gently spread my legs as he nodded. And that's when I realized what he meant.

"Oh," I blurted.

His grin went devilish as he focused his attention on my breasts. He kissed and licked each nipple in turn. "What did you think I meant?"

"To be honest...I forgot that 'eating' was even an option." I realized how stupid I must have sounded. But it had been so long since I'd been appreciated. Or desired. Or *taken care of* like this. I could count on one hand how many times Jericho even remembered I had a clit. And I had a sneaking suspicion that was going to be Troy's first priority.

It was almost embarrassing how different they were. Because it meant that I had been accepting crumbs from Jericho for longer than I even wanted to admit.

A sigh rippled out of him. "I don't understand how a man could look at this beautiful pussy and *not* get hungry." He captured my lips in a kiss and then his mouth began trailing downward. I watched him in a state of shock. And then awe. And then I wasn't watching him at all, because once his tongue found the crease of my pussy, my eyes fluttered shut.

Troy held my ass cheeks in his big, powerful hands while he feasted. He licked and sucked and worshipped my pussy in a way that I'd only ever heard about. I clutched his head between my legs, letting myself get washed away in the sensation of his tongue laving over my clit.

All the air in my lungs came out in a big whoosh.

He moaned into my pussy. "You taste so fucking good Maddie." His tongue plunged inside me. I squeaked, gripping the top of his head.

"I can tell how much you like it too." He flicked his tongue back and forth over my clit, grunting with pleasure. "You're fucking dripping."

My mouth fell open as I tried to make any sort of response. None came. He jerked me closer to his mouth and I propped myself up, hands behind me, giving in to the ridiculousness of it all.

Yes, I could orgasm on the kitchen island.

Troy seemed intent on making sure I did. I arched my back, opening myself up wider to him, a long, low moan ripping out of me as everything went hot and buzzy inside my body. I moaned indecently, far noisier than I could ever remember being, but when this man's tongue was fucking me without pause, there was no other response. I squeezed his head between my knees as my belly trembled. Then the orgasm popped, bright waves of pleasure exploding inside me.

He licked at my clit until the pleasure faded and I was left laughing and stroking his head. He grinned, his mouth slick from *me*.

"You are so fucking sexy, Maddie." He pressed a kiss to my inner thigh, not releasing me quite yet. "Do you have any idea?"

"I don't," I admitted with a laugh. "As sexy as you are when you wear the gray sweatpants?"

He paused his kisses. "You like those?"

"Love them."

"Noted." Troy kissed his way down my legs until he hit my knees. "You are delicious. But we should go somewhere else for what comes next."

"The kitchen island isn't good for that?" I teased.

"You need to be more comfortable when all the pounding starts." His cocky grin made me burst into laughter. I was on cloud nine after that orgasm. I'd never seen such a perfect, hilarious, sexy man. He slid me off the island into his arms, and when I looked back at where I'd been sitting, he tutted. "Don't go into caretaker mode. We'll take care of that later, because right now, I'm taking care of *you*."

If I hadn't fallen in love with him already, that line did it. I giggled, wrapping my legs around his waist as he carried me across the cabin and up the stairs to the loft. But I sensed the catch of his breath as we went up the steps. The way he seemed to wince when he used that knee.

"I'm too heavy," I told him. But when I tried to wriggle free, his grip only tightened around me.

"You're not," he growled.

"Then your knee hurts you and you won't admit it," I accused him. I'd seen the hit he took with that baseball bat. Part of me wasn't sure how he could still walk at all.

"It's fine." His fingertips dug into the soft flesh of my thighs as he stepped into the loft. "God you feel fucking good with your legs wrapped around me. It makes everything else feel better." His perfect lips found mine again for a scorching yet tender kiss before reluctantly placing me on the perfectly made queen bed.

"Finally I get to test out your bed," I teased, shifting uncomfortably. The navy comforter was pulled taut—no doubt a remnant of his former military life—but all I could think about was the cleanup. The *stains* we might make.

"What's wrong?" He stood at the end of the bed, towering over me, as he grabbed my chin and directed my gaze up toward him.

I opened my mouth but couldn't find the words. It was embarrassing—how much of a *mom* I was. Always thinking about the consequences. What came next. What else needed to be done.

"I was thinking about how we're gonna mess up this perfect comforter because we're gonna get sex juice all over Lenny's nice things and I don't want to be a bad guest."

The most heartbreaking grin broke out on Troy's face. He cupped my face in his big, rough hands. "Just when I think you can't get any sweeter, you say something like that."

I laughed self-consciously. "I don't want to take his generosity for granted."

"I promise, you're not. If nothing else, you can blame anything you want on me. But I'll clean up the perfect comforter when we're done. He'll never know."

"I can help—"

"I want you to not think about it. Let me do it, babe."

A happy sigh escaped me. Those two sentences might have been the hottest thing anyone had ever said to me. Probably the first time a man had implored me to set down the weight of the world.

Did Troy realize how hot that was? How uncommon?

I wanted to know, but all my thoughts dissolved as he laced his fingers through my left hand, lifting my arm to inspect it. Then he pressed his lips to my forearm—right where the bruises had been that he'd spotted the week before.

"But I do want to be absolutely clear about one thing." His kisses trailed down my arm, to the back of my hand. "We're gonna get sex juice everywhere."

I dissolved into laughter and he released me long enough to shimmy out of his jeans. Slate gray boxers barely contained the thick ridge of his arousal. He tugged his t-shirt off next, revealing his wide shoulders and neatly trimmed, black chest hair.

"Oh my God." I smoothed my hands over the expanse of skin—his strong chest, down the ripples of his abs, along the waistband of his boxer briefs. He was sexier than I'd imagined.

He watched me with hooded eyes. "Go on. See what you do to me."

I tugged down his boxer briefs, revealing the thick shaft of his cock. It bobbed heavily in front of him as he stepped out of his briefs. I wrapped my fingers around his cock, eyeing the swollen head, the veins popping out along the shaft. I didn't normally find cocks *attractive* but his was an exception. I covered the thick head with my mouth, my tongue finding his salty precum. A low hum escaped him as I learned the contours of his cockhead, taking him deep into my mouth, as far as I could go without choking.

Troy grunted, his fingers knotting into my hair.

"Your mouth feels so fucking good around my cock." His voice was low, controlled, but barely. His cock slid farther down my throat, so far that I almost gagged. I felt him harden further. "Oh, fuck yes, Maddie."

Having this wall of man in front of me, filling my mouth, was hot—and equally hot to imagine what we might look like from the outside. I wished there was a mirror in the bedroom so that I could see us. Especially what was about to come. I clenched my legs together, pulling away from his cock.

"I need you inside me." I'd never been so demanding in the bedroom before, but I needed him. *Now*. Troy cradled the sides of my face, looking absolutely drugged.

"I don't have a condom." His lips brushed against mine.

"I don't care." If I didn't get this man inside me, I'd go crazy. "I'm on birth control, and I'm clean. Are you?"

He nodded, searching my face. "Clean. But not on birth control."

Laughter rolled out of me, and the grin that lit up his face made me fall in love with him for one brief, wild moment. I scooted back on the bed and Troy eased onto the comforter, his knees denting the bed on either side of me. He lowered himself onto me, his rigid cock finding the heat between my legs. I arched into him, clutching at his broad shoulders, needing so much more. This felt like my first time all over again, and in a way, it was—the first time I'd ever felt this way about someone. The first time I'd craved it with every cell of my body. The first time I thought I'd lose my mind if I didn't get it.

The head of his cock slipped past my folds as he pushed inside me. My eyes fluttered shut, a low moan ripping out of me as he sank deep inside me. I felt my walls clamp around him, swallowing him, begging for more of him. Troy buried his face in the hollow of my neck, gripping the sides of my rib cage like he was worried I might drift away.

"Jesus, Maddie. You feel amazing." He scooped his hands beneath my back, erasing every inch of space between us as he pushed into me, again and again. "Better than a perfect ten."

His comment made me grin so hard my cheeks hurt.

"Takes one to know one," I told him, my breath wispy and faint. The feel of him stretching me, filling me, was the only thing I could focus on. He thrusted with so much energy I felt like he might burst through my low back. I clung to him, welcoming all of it, my nails sinking into the ridge of his shoulder.

"I'm close, babe." He growled into my collarbone, which caused a fascinating ripple of muscles along his back as he pounded into me. I was close to coming too—*again.* He reached his hand between us, fingers rubbing against my clit in circles. The friction pushed me back to the edge, and all the way past it. For the second time that night. I clenched and moaned, the high even higher this time now that he was filling me to the brim. I called out his name, repeating it without meaning to, practically like a chant.

"Ohhhh, Maddie."

The heat of his release filled me, and he stilled once his cock had stopped spasming. He searched my face, something unreadable in his gaze.

I smoothed my hands over his broad, warm chest, still struggling to catch my breath. I loved the feel of him still inside me. In fact, I loved everything about this.

"You're fucking incredible, you know that?" Troy snagged my lips in a tender kiss. "I think hearing you come is my new favorite thing."

I was still too stupefied to be embarrassed by a comment like that. I couldn't even lift my arms, much less blush. Instead, I laughed.

With Troy, it felt easy. I could break myself open and trust that he'd accept it. Like it, even.

I wanted more of it. More of *him.*

So much more than I even wanted to admit to myself.

CHAPTER ELEVEN

TROY

"All right, girls. Have a good day." I leaned across the empty passenger seat of my Jeep, waving out the open window as Maddie and Grace held hands and walked toward the school building in the pre-dawn morning. They both looked back at me, grinning and waving, bundled up in their winter coats.

"Go get that knee checked out," she said sternly.

I grunted. "We'll see."

Maddie held my gaze and I winked at her. I couldn't tell if the ruddiness of her cheeks was from a blush or the winter wind.

I waited in the drop-off line until they disappeared inside the building. Grace's daycare was in a section of the multi-use building. I relaxed once they were inside—safe, for now. I smiled to myself as I pulled away, some distant part of me wondering who the hell I was becoming.

Dropping off your girls for school? My blinker ticked as I waited at the intersection. *Scheduling your day around school pick up?*

The words almost didn't make sense to me. But it was all I wanted to be doing right now.

I needed to leave for New York by that weekend. So we had at least four days ahead of us to play house and see how things progressed with Jericho. What scared me was what came after I left for Ecuador. Jericho didn't seem like a guy who would just roll over because a bodyguard stole his baseball bat during an aggressive encounter. Maddie needed a plan...and I intended on helping her create one.

As promised, I spent the day taking care of Maddie's car. I got it moved safely to her parents' house, fresh tires and all, and caught a ride share back to the garage to pick up my own car since her parents were working. Then I spent the rest of the day getting things for the cabin during a grocery store run, including a weird cheese board for Maddie and some new coloring books and crayons for Grace.

Because my girls need a treat.

There it was again. That inner voice saying some wild things.

I wasn't sure when things had gone from 'just checking on Mercedes' family' to 'my girls', but I suspected it had something to do with that Christmas party. I couldn't fucking deny it. I'd fallen for Maddie the second I saw her.

Once three-thirty hit, it was time to pick up Maddie and Grace. I crept through the school pick-up lane, looking around at all the other parents in mini-vans and SUVs. In all my assignments around the globe, I'd never found myself in a school pick-up line before. I tapped the steering wheel as the line moved forward, imperceptibly slow. I scanned the faces of the kids streaming out of the building, heading toward cars, the frazzled pickup attendants trying to keep everyone in order. As I got closer to the school, I heard a shout. Then a *tap-tap-tap* at the passenger door. Maddie ran up a moment later, looking spooked.

"Gracie, I told you not to run off like that." She hoisted Grace into her arms from beneath my line of sight. Grace beamed at me through the passenger side window and I leaned over to push the door open for them.

"Hey girls. How was your day?"

Grace hopped into the car, throwing her arms around my neck. "Toy!"

I touched her arm gently, looking over at Maddie. Something warm and bubbly sprang to life in my chest. So this was what I'd been missing out on by avoiding settling down. I swallowed hard, not wanting to think about that right now.

"You have a good day, monkey?" I'd started calling her monkey ever since the Twisty Monkey game. She nodded eagerly, dawdling on the center console.

"Grace, we need to get you in your car seat sweetie," Maddie urged gently, looking behind us. "The others are waiting for their turn and they can get pretty feisty."

"Do what your mama says," I told Grace, jerking my head to the backseat. "We're gonna go back to the cabin and we can catch up there."

"Okay." Grace clambered into the backseat, and Maddie snapped her into the car seat from the rear door. As she was finishing up, Grace added, "I missed you, Toy."

There was that damn bubbly sensation again. Fuck if it didn't make my chest a little tight—because I'd also missed her.

"I missed you too, monkey." I looked at her in the rearview mirror as Maddie slid into the front seat, tugging her door shut. To her, I said, "I missed you too."

Maddie sent me a shy grin as she buckled up. "Well I'm glad you admitted that first, so I don't sound like the clingy one."

A laugh rocketed out of me. I eased out of the pick-up line as I shook my head. "I'll take the fall. It's fine. As long as I know I'm not the only one thinking it."

"You aren't." And she sent me a smile that was so pretty I wanted to take a picture of it. To remember not just her, but this moment, and the whole visit to Kentucky. "And speaking of taking a fall...did you get that knee checked out?"

"No. I was too busy with other stuff. And I didn't fall," I corrected. "I got hit with a bat."

"You took the fall for *me*," she pointed out.

I held out my hand, inviting her to give me hers as I drove. "You're right. And I'd do it again." She slipped hers into my big palm and I pulled it into my lap. And that's when I knew the answer to my question:

Just like that.

That was how fast things had gone from 'Mercedes' family' to 'my girls'.

Something about Maddie clicked into place, just like that, and I wasn't the only one who felt it.

One full week beneath Len's buckhorn chandelier was all it took to turn me into a family man. Each day of the school routine cemented me a little further into this new role. Was I a stay at home bodyguard now? An alpha homemaker who made dinner for his girls every night? I didn't know what the appropriate term was for this new phase of my life, but I knew one thing: I didn't exactly want it to end.

But the deadline was fast approaching. After a whirlwind week of school drop offs and pickups, followed by lots of play time, family dinner, and then the hottest lovemaking this side of the Appalachian mountains, I couldn't even remember who I'd been when I showed up in Louisville. By Friday evening, as I unveiled that night's dinner of ribeye, garlic mashed potatoes, and steamed broccoli, all I could think about was that this was our last full day together before I needed to drop the girls off and head north.

And I was fucking sad about it, but determined not to let it upend our last moments together.

"Where's my girlies at? Time to eat." My voice boomed through the cabin, and then the giggles came. Gracie-bell loved it when I called her to dinner each night, always in a new way. She scampered into the kitchen, abandoning the work she and her mom were doing in the great room tending the fireplace.

"Oh my God, Troy," Maddie murmured as her gaze fell on the carefully arranged plates, each one with a showstopping ribeye. "You're incredible."

"Had to go all out for our last meal at the cabin."

My words fell like dead weight between us. The stool creaked as she eased onto it, and we shared a look.

"Toy take me to school tomorrow?" Grace asked, looking between us as she settled into her seat.

"Honey, we don't have school tomorrow." Maddie pressed a kiss to the top of her daughter's head then put herself at eye-level with Grace. "But tomorrow we are going back to Nana and Buppa's house."

"To live there?" Grace wobbily maneuvered a spoon of pota-toes into her mouth.

"Yes, honey, to live there."

"With Toy?"

"No, honey. Not with Troy." Maddie stroked her daughter's hair while an enormous pout erupted on Grace's face.

"But why not?" Grace whined.

Maddie sent me a panicked look. She tucked Grace against her and mouthed to me, "I knew this would happen."

"I'll see you another time, Gracie-bell." I rubbed her back, unsure what to say to a sad three year old. Her concept of time was tenuous at best. "It won't be long. I promise."

Grace pouted, begrudgingly accepting spoonfuls of mashed potato as Maddie fed her. But she never gave up the crossed arms or scowl.

Maddie maneuvered the conversation away from the topic of *what came next*, for Grace's sake. We chatted about anything and everything else, until Grace was ready to go back to her coloring books leaving me and Maddie facing each other with empty plates between us.

A moment of silence passed between us.

"Is it wrong to be this sad that I have to go back to real life tomorrow?" Maddie punctuated it with a laugh, but the smile faded fast.

"Not wrong." I moved into the seat closer to her, where Grace had been sitting. I faced her, pulling her hands into mine. "I don't want to go back to real life either. But I do want to make sure you're going to be okay when we do."

"I'll be fine at my parents' house," she said. "I won't lie, I'd be a little nervous if I lived on my own right now. But they'll be with me each night."

"And then let's go over the plan again." We'd been figuring out the specific steps for what came next, as well as contingency plans, when it came to Jericho. She'd done the hardest parts—initiating the separation, hiring the divorce lawyer, waiting the requisite year to formally file. But the longer Jericho dragged his heels, the more gray area he had to do something unhinged. I wanted him excised from her life like a nasty mole.

"Once I'm back in town, I'm filing a report about the car. Then I'm meeting with my lawyer again to talk about going through with the uncontested divorce." She ticked off her fingers as she spoke. "Then we'll draft the custodial plan. If Jericho tries anything again, that's when I file the police report and request an order of protection."

I nodded as she spoke, encouraging her as she ran down the action plan. Hearing this felt good—but it didn't entirely appease me.

"And what if he tries to lay a finger on you again?" I asked.

Her throat bobbed, looking at me with hooded eyes. "I call the cops. And then I call you."

"Good girl."

The flush in her neck told me she liked that. I smoothed my hand up her arms and then jerked the seat of her stool closer to me in one swift movement. Our knees knocked, but I folded her between my legs, hugging her as close as I could.

"I think I'll start looking for my own place soon," Maddie said, nibbling on her bottom lip. "My parents have been nice enough to let us stay with them as I got back on my feet. They want me to save for a downpayment so I can buy my own house, which I've been doing. When I'm not paying legal fees that is. But I don't know...I was thinking I might start looking for an apartment to rent sooner."

"If that's what you want," I smoothed my lips across her forehead, "then that's what you should do."

She nodded, but she didn't look convinced.

"I should do what's smart," she finally said.

"Unless you have a different idea?"

She fiddled with the buttons on my flannel button-up. "There's a lot of things I want that don't make sense."

I felt that statement in every cell of my body right now. I wanted Maddie and Grace to be a part of my life, even though I couldn't offer what they needed most: a homebase. Stability. Permanence. It felt silly to even think about a future with Maddie.

But I also couldn't imagine a future without her.

"Like what?" I prompted, wondering if she had the same thing on her mind.

She looked away, seeming to wrestle with something. Before she could answer, Grace scampered over, pushing the newest coloring book page up to our level. Maddie's face lit up as she beheld her daughter's work, and I admired it too, genuinely impressed with the attempt to color inside the lines.

"You've gotten better at this since we've been at the cabin," I told her.

"For you, Toy." She held it out to me so I could rip the page out—something of our ritual already—which meant that it was officially mine. I had five other pictures just like it behind magnets on the fridge.

"Thank you, monkey." I dutifully ripped it out and set it aside, handing her the coloring book back. But she wasn't satisfied until I ceremoniously hung the picture on the fridge. The stool creaked as I slid away from Maddie, leading Grace over to the fridge so she could select the magnet and the best spot for the new picture. Once all that was done, she happily skipped back to her coloring station in the great room.

"Where were we?" I eased back onto the stool, pulling Maddie right back to where she'd been tucked between my legs. She giggled, nuzzling up to me. "I believe you were saying the not-smart things that you want."

She sighed, shaking her head. "I need to focus on the smart things."

"Let's just *hear* what you think is out of reach."

She paused, studying a faraway point across the cabin. "I want to get out of Kentucky."

Wasn't quite what I'd been hoping to hear but I liked it all the same. "And why does that seem out of reach?"

"My teaching certification is for Kentucky," she admitted. "And I need my job. I need to keep Grace in her daycare. She's happy where she is."

I nodded, mulling over the information. "Well, I do have an alternative idea for you. You could always roam the US in an RV and ruin Grace's childhood."

Maddie burst into laughter, swatting my chest. "Thank you for the suggestion. Though I'm pretty sure you've already explained to me why I *shouldn't* do that."

"Just wanted you to be aware of your options." I gathered her against me, more than ready for the adult portion of the evening. But we had some time before Grace went to bed still. "I'll think on it. I know there's something perfect out there for you, Maddie."

What I didn't understand was why deep down, I thought that maybe I could be that perfect thing for her.

I didn't have a home; not even a lease. I had my Jeep and a few duffel bags of shit. Who was I kidding?

I needed to listen to Maddie's words. I needed to do the smart thing.

And that meant continuing my path as I'd planned all along.

CHAPTER TWELVE

TROY

I awoke before my alarm—six-twenty.

I knew why.

Maddie.

I stared up at the criss-crossing beams of the cabin roof. She'd been spending each night in my bed this week, slipping out in the early morning hours to return to her bed with Grace. I was used to rousing when she slipped out, but today was different.

This was the last morning. The absolute end.

Sadness washed over me. I turned onto my side, facing Maddie as she slept. My gaze drifted from her long, dark lashes to the faintest hint of freckles across her cheeks, along the wisps of dark chocolate hair that framed her face. She stirred slightly, and I took this as my sign to get her up for the day.

I dragged my fingertips along the curve of her cheek, trying to absorb as much of *this* as I could.

"Time to get up," I whispered, pressing a soft kiss to her forehead.

I liked taking care of her and Grace. It felt good—natural, somehow. I'd never seen myself as a husband or daddy, but these eight days in Len's cabin had got me thinking.

She mumbled something unintelligible. I wrapped my arms around her, placing soft kisses along her jawline. Maddie drew a deep breath, burrowing into me. My eyes drifted shut. I could have stayed there forever.

But she moved against me in just the right way. My cock perked up, ready for fun. I nuzzled into the hollow of her neck, searching out that perfect scent.

I don't want this to end.

They were the words I was afraid to say. I had no right to say them, not when Maddie and Grace had needs, and I had an ever-changing location. My next stop was Ecuador. And after that? Uncharted.

The least sexiest thing to say to a single mom.

She giggled as I nuzzled her, burrowing harder against me. "Good morning to you."

"Let's make it a better morning." I bit softly into the side of her neck, dragging my tongue along her sweet skin. She shivered, those pretty hazel eyes fluttering open as I smoothed my hand along her curves and in between her legs. My fingers danced over the crotch of her panties, already finding damp heat waiting for me. I pressed my fingers beneath the fabric, smoothing over the tight nub of her clit.

A sigh shuddered out of her at the same time my feral mode kicked in. Good lord, this woman was juicy. From head to toe.

"You feel so fucking perfect." I slipped my finger into her pussy. "How are you this wet already?"

She laughed. "I sleep next to you, remember?"

I silenced the compliment with a kiss, moving my finger in and out of her slowly, up to pinch her clit, then back inside. She moved against my hand, urging more friction. My cock stiffened the more she moaned and whimpered. Her thighs clenched around my hand.

"God damn, Maddie." I snagged her lips in a deep kiss as I rolled on top of her. She smoothed her hands over my bare chest, bleary eyed and beautiful. I pushed my hands underneath her sleep shirt, palming the big handfuls of her tits. "What a way to wake up."

"You're better than coffee," she teased, clamping her legs around my waist.

"That's a high compliment, coming from you." I tugged her panties down, until they flew across the loft. "If that's true, how can you live without me?"

I'd meant the question as something innocent and playful, but as soon as the words tumbled out, I realized how serious they were. Because this was the end, and somehow, we had to go our separate ways.

Something heavy crossed her face, but it didn't last long. I made sure of it. I pulled off my boxer briefs, letting them join her panties across the loft, and then eased myself inside her. Stretching her, deliciously slowly, until we both forgot anything that had existed before *this*.

I couldn't see anything beyond her hazel eyes as I pushed into her, over and over again. Her fingernails dug into my biceps. Her pussy walls clamped around me at the same time my balls tightened and the coil of pleasure released. Heat swarmed my body as I released inside her, her low moans filling the cabin loft.

Maddie was jello when we were done. Once we'd cuddled and laughed together for a few minutes, I scooped her into my arms and carried her to the bathroom.

"Troy," she hissed, swatting at my arms. "Put me down. I'm too heavy."

I tutted. "I don't make it a habit of telling beautiful women this, but you're wrong."

She laughed, wriggling out of my arms in the bathroom. "You shouldn't carry anything heavy with an injured knee you refuse to get checked out."

I bit at my bottom lip as my gaze followed the delectable curve of her ass. "It's fine. Remember what I said? You make it fine."

She expelled a burst of air that sounded equal parts frustrated and amused. I gave her a cheesy grin in return. Truth was, my knee still hurt. And sometimes, it locked up. *No bueno.* But my approach was to ignore it until it resolved on its own. Besides, I had way more important things to tend to while Maddie was with me. I didn't plan on giving away a second of my time to anything that wasn't *my girls.*

Maddie and I made quick work of cleaning up, then she slipped down the stairs to return to her own bed for when Grace woke up. And I got to continuing my day like I always did: with exercise.

I was determined to keep my routine the same. Not just today, but in general. I only looked ahead.

No matter how much it gnawed at me.

As the morning wore on, I tried my best to click into gear for what came next. Nash Nightingale's new assignment. The trip to Ecuador—which started *tomorrow.* Conjuring any sort of excitement about the gig was impossible because I couldn't yank my attention from Maddie. Not when I was sharing my last breakfast with her and Grace, and thinking about what might happen while I was gone. Maddie got to tidying the kitchen after breakfast while I loaded their bags into the Jeep. When I came inside the cabin, Grace was hopping around, ready for one last round of Twisty Monkey.

I was happy to oblige. Because who knew when I'd be able to again?

After five—okay, six—near-puke inducing rounds of Twisty Monkey, the worst and best game ever invented by accident, Maddie and Grace waited in the Jeep while I closed up the cabin. I sent Len a quick text to let him know we left, pausing before I could add anything else. I didn't want to say I fell in love under his buckhorn chandelier or anything, but I felt like Len needed to know that I'd definitely fallen for someone in there. Maybe later, after I dropped off the girls, I could admit to someone what was happening inside my chest.

Since it wasn't a school day, I drove to Maddie's parents' house. Grace got excited as she recognized the neighborhood.

"We see Nana!" She clapped.

"Yes, sweetie. It's time to see Nana." Maddie unbuckled her seat belt slowly, looking over at me. Grace made a racket kicking and wriggling in the car seat, wanting to be unbuckled so she could go inside. Maddie slipped out of the car to release Grace, and her daughter bounded up to the front door.

"You think she'll forget about me?" I asked Maddie, who sank back into the front seat once Grace had gone inside the house with her grandparents.

"No. She'll probably talk about you for the next year."

Silence settled between us. It was almost awkward, the first time I'd felt that way around Maddie since meeting her. I didn't know what to say. Where to even begin. She nibbled on her lip as she looked over at me.

"Will *you* forget about me?" I could barely force the words past my lips.

"Never." There was no hesitation in her voice. Only a challenge.

One that I wasn't sure I could meet.

"Gonna talk about me for a year too, huh?" I squeezed her hand, hoping to see a smile at my corny joke. I got one, but it didn't last long.

"You should go." She looked toward the front door. "You have such a long drive. All I can think about is how you'll have to drive straight through if I keep you any longer."

She wasn't wrong. But I wasn't quite ready to leave yet, either.

"I don't need many breaks. I could probably do the whole trip in one go." But the subtext behind her comment stuck with me. Reminding me of the truth: this was the end. I reached for her hand, giving it a quick squeeze. "What's the plan, again?"

She offered me a warm smile. "File the report about the car. Meet with the lawyer. Work on the uncontested divorce. Follow up with you about what the doctor said about your knee."

I fought a grin. "You're really not gonna let me get away with ignoring it, huh?"

"Nope. So if you want me to follow the plan…then you should follow it, too."

I nodded, finally realizing that she wasn't going to drop it. Because she was right…and we both knew it. "Okay. But I want it to go on the record that I'm only doing this because you're the most beautiful woman I've ever laid eyes on."

"Noted. And thank you." Her hazel gaze twinkled as she leaned forward and pressed a kiss to my lips.

When she pulled away, her gaze slid to the front door of her parents' house. Her mother poked her head out, looking toward the Jeep. Grace hopped at her feet. They were waiting for Maddie. But I wasn't quite ready to end this.

"I should go," she started.

I opened my mouth to say something—*can we keep talking? What if I flew back to see you after Ecuador? Are you open to long distance with a guy like me?*—but none of the words materialized. I had no idea how to launch this conversation.

"Thanks for everything, Troy," she said, leaning over the console to throw her arms around me. I held her against me, my heart pounding against my ribs. This couldn't be it.

Yet it had to be.

She slipped out of the Jeep before I could get my brain back to working order. As soon as the door shut behind her, sadness prickled through me, even though I didn't want to admit it. It was time to leave. My path was set. I needed to accept it and get on with it.

I backed out of the driveway before I could do anything stupid, like walk up to her parents' house and introduce myself as her boyfriend. I drove to the nearest gas station, my attention wandering as I filled up my tank.

Would one last good-bye hug be so bad?

Leaving now felt wrong somehow. I had a strange feeling in my gut that I didn't like. One that I knew better than to ignore.

Once I was done pumping gas, I eased back into the driver's seat and called Maddie. I didn't care that it might make me look lovesick or smitten or any of those things I didn't want to be but already knew I was.

"Hello?" I could hear the smile in her voice.

"Hey you. How you doing?"

She laughed softly. "Just fine. Same as when you dropped me off fifteen minutes ago."

"Yeah, I figured. Just wanted to check in."

"Are you going to be calling me every fifteen minutes while you're gone?"

"If you don't mind," I teased. "I like to get frequent updates."

"I suppose I could arrange some sort of live cam..."

I cleared my throat. "After hours style or what?"

"That would be a first for me, but it could be arranged."

The sexy lilt of her voice had me grinning like a fool. "You sure you don't want me to come back over there? I could stay a few more days."

She sighed. "Troy, you need to get to New York and catch your plane. You're leaving the country tomorrow."

"You're right." I studied the leather braiding of the steering wheel as I fumbled for what my next words would be. "But it feels wrong leaving you and Grace behind."

"Believe me, we wish you could stay. But we'll be fine. I promise you."

I drew a deep breath, trying to believe her words.

"Hey Maddie…" I looked around the barren gas station, trying to figure out if I really had the words inside me. Maddie screamed roots, and I'd never had them. But something about her made me want to try growing them. "If there was some chance that I…I don't know…might come back through Louisville on my way back from Ecuador…"

"Mm-hmm…."

"And I could work it out where I swung by…we don't need to stay in the cabin, I'm not saying you go back to the cabin or anything…"

She laughed softly, reminding me how I still hadn't gotten to the damn point.

"Well, Grace would need a few rounds of Twisty Monkey, you know?" I rubbed at the back of my neck. I'd never felt so inarticulate in my entire life. "Maybe we could…you know…I don't know…"

Now she was full-blown laughing. At *me*. "Troy, what are you trying to say? Just spit it out."

"I…" I drew a deep breath. I'd lived through boot camp, tours of duty, protecting high-profile political figures, and I'd even been involved in a few shoot-outs in my time. Nothing came close to this: admitting to a woman that despite my best efforts, she owned my heart. "I want to make sure you'll be okay. But it's more than that. Way more. I know I can't fix everything…but I want to help you carry the load. I don't think I can go to Ecuador without knowing that I'm going to see you again as soon as humanly possible."

The other end of the line was quiet for a moment, but then I heard what sounded like sniffles.

"Troy." There was so much emotion in her voice. I'd never loved the sound of my name so much from anyone's lips. "That's all I want too. I was too afraid to ask. I know you have a busy schedule…I didn't want to get in the way."

"You'd never be in the way. Hell, it's everything else that's in the way. We'll figure it out. We will." The words landed like a hammer. There was no questioning it. We would figure it out because I didn't want the alternative of not knowing when I'd see her next.

"Yeah. We'll figure it out." I could hear the smile in her voice, and see it in my mind's eye. I was ready to drive back to her parents' house for one last hug, which she must have been able to sense. "Are you driving north yet?"

"Just finishing up getting gas. I'm about to call Nash with my ETA. Tell my monkey Gracie-bell I miss her already."

"I will."

"And I'll show you how much I miss you already when I call you later from my bedroom."

Her sweet laughter was cut short by a soft gasp.

"What's wrong?" The hairs on the back of my neck stood up as I turned the engine.

"Oh my God," Maddie murmured. Nothing about her voice sounded good. "Oh my God you've gotta be kidding me."

Now my gut was a complete knot. "Maddie, what is it?"

"Jericho just showed up."

CHAPTER THIRTEEN
MADDIE

"Mommy, is Toy coming?"

Grace's sweet voice broke my concentration as I stared out the bedroom window overlooking the driveway. Jericho's Lexus blocked all the cars in the driveway from the ridiculous angle he'd parked. I could see the sliver of his dark blond hair from the window as he stood on the porch at the front door.

I slipped my phone into the back pocket of my jeans as Troy had instructed. And then I kicked into gear.

"Honey, I want you to go play." I didn't know what Jericho wanted, other than to make my life harder. But both my parents were downstairs. This could still end well. I simply wanted to make sure Grace didn't suspect anything was amiss for now. But maybe she could already tell.

She whimpered as I guided her out of the bedroom and into the spare room that we'd set up as her play room. "Mommy, what's happening?"

"Nothing, sweetie." She had to be sensing my anxiety spike somehow. I drew a deep breath, trying to keep my voice level, carefree. "I just think it's time to play for now. Can you stay in here and play for a little bit? I want you to color me a tree."

She blinked up at me with wide, worried eyes. "A tree?"

"Yes, honey. A tree." I got down on her level, offering her a big smile while I rubbed the sides of her arms. From downstairs, I heard undertones of stomping and a male voice. *Fuck.* "Draw me the prettiest tree you can think of, okay? I really want a picture of a pretty tree."

She nodded hesitantly.

"But do not come out of this room, okay?" There was more stomping from downstairs, and I could barely keep my worries at bay. I needed to get down there, but not with Grace. "I need you to stay in this room and play."

"Okay, Mommy," she whispered.

I kissed the top of her head and slipped out of the room, pulling the door shut behind me. Sounds of an argument drifted into the hallway from downstairs. My stomach wrenched and I hurried to the stairs, determined to see this through. Jericho wasn't going away. We needed to take care of this once and for all, so our family could find the new norm.

That was my only wish.

As soon as my feet hit the ground floor, I spotted Jericho in the front hall. Both of my parents were there, looking worried.

"There she is," Jericho sneered. He looked ready for the office, his dark blond tresses slicked back and his khaki slacks and light blue button up pressed neatly. But something dark twisted his classically handsome features. I wasn't sure if it had always been there, or if it had just emerged since he'd gotten the divorce papers. But I barely recognized this man...even after having been married to him for almost five years.

"Jericho, why don't we take this conversation outside?" my father suggested. He was a 6'1, broad-shouldered former football player who commanded respect, but something in Jericho's stance suggested he'd throw a punch at anyone right now. Even my mother.

"I just want to talk to Maddie." His gaze zeroed in on me. "You've been avoiding me."

"I wasn't avoiding you." I didn't budge from the foot of the staircase. There were three people between him and Grace, and it needed to stay that way. "I've been busy."

"I deserve to see my daughter."

"Then you can sign the papers and we'll set up a custodial arrangement." I crossed my arms over my chest, partly to hide the fact that my heart was racing a mile a minute. Like this would somehow bolster my confidence. I could hear Troy's voice in my head. *What's the plan, babe?* "If you don't sign the papers, I'll be moving forward with the divorce anyway. But you have to do your part if you want to get custodial rights."

"I don't need a judge to tell me whether or not I can see my own *daughter*," he spat. "That's bullshit."

"It's not bullshit, it's how it works." I tried to hide the waver in my voice. "We're not together anymore, so we need to set up parameters."

"Parameters?" His bitter laugh nearly burned my skin. "I see. So you can run off with your little boyfriend while you're still legally married? Sounds like something a fucking whore would do. I'm not playing your mind games, Maddie."

"Jericho, you're not going to speak like that inside my house." My father's voice landed like a hammer and he moved to push Jericho toward the door.

"You should leave now," my mother said firmly.

"What did I say?" The hint of a smile twisted at his lips. "Come on guys. I said it sounded like something a whore *would* do, I never said Maddie *was* a whore. Even if it's exactly what she fucking did. You guys can draw your own conclusions."

My stomach twisted. Those types of mind games he accused me of were exactly the type he loved to play in our relationship. Just being reminded of the circular logic made me sick. The only way out was to not respond directly to it.

"Nothing to say, huh?" Jericho nodded my way as my father stood in front of him, urging him toward the door.

"I'll give you ten seconds to leave on your own," my father warned.

"The fact that she's not even defending herself says it all, don't you think?" Jericho was unfazed. "Doesn't sound like a very fit mother to me. Do you want your granddaughter being raised by someone who breaks the sanctity of marriage? She and I exchanged vows. And still she ran off with some man and probably got railed all weekend like a slut."

"Jericho," my father warned. "This is your last chance to leave peacefully."

"I don't want to leave peacefully." His voice was rising now. "I want to take my daughter and get the fuck out of here. I don't trust you people. Least of all *her*."

I straightened my back, rejecting all of the hurtful words he spewed. I willed them to roll off my body, like oil separating from water. "Jericho, you need to leave right now. Everything else will be figured out by the courts. You're not taking Grace with you."

"Like hell I'm not." He stepped forward but my father hooked him by the arm, keeping him at bay for only a few moments. But the longer he was detained, the harder Jericho struggled.

"You're not going to keep me from what I want," he growled, snagging his arm back. My mom held up her hands.

"Jericho, think about what you're doing," she pleaded.

"If you take another step, I'm calling the cops," I warned him.

"I don't give a fuck what you do. I'm taking my daughter." Jericho barreled past my father, who shouted and lunged for Jericho. But Jericho darted away, eluding his grasp, and stormed toward me.

"Jericho, stop!" My voice came out shrill, betraying every ounce of fear that I felt. Before Jericho reached me, my father grabbed at his shoulders, hauling him back. Jericho swung his fist as he turned, landing a solid punch to my father's face. His gruff shout filled the front hall.

"Jericho! What has gotten into you?" my mother screamed.

"I'm calling the police." My announcement withered in the chaos now filling the living room. But I didn't reach for my cell phone. Even amid my frozen limbs and high anxiety, I remembered what I was supposed to do. I reached for the telephone on the small table near the landing, but Jericho reached it first.

"The fuck you are." He swatted the phone out of my hand so forcefully the entire thing toppled to the floor. "Besides, it won't even matter. You think I don't know enough of the police force? That I don't have them in my back pocket?" His smile grew sinister. "Get out of my fucking way. I'm taking Grace now."

"No you aren't!" My voice trembled. I had no way to stop him, and he knew it.

He tipped his head, a creepy smile twisting at his lips. "Yes I am."

Time. I just needed more time. That's all I could think about. "You're not going up there, Jericho. If you try anything at all, you'll never get custodial rights. The fact that you just punched my dad has you fucked. And you know it. Think clearly, please!"

"I'm thinking clearly for the first time in my life." His words fell like a threat and when he stepped forward, I didn't budge. "Get. Out. Of. My. Way." Jericho shoved me aside, and even though I'd braced myself, I toppled under the angry force. I hit the wall hard with my shoulder and lost my balance, sliding to the floor, but I kicked my leg out to trip him as he headed for the stairs.

Jericho stumbled over my feet, swearing loudly. "You fucking whore."

He glanced behind him, finding my parents distracted with my father's bloody nose and potentially broken nose. Jericho grabbed me by the hair and brought his face close to mine.

"I should have fucking done this years ago," he hissed, and then he slammed my head into the wall.

Everything went black.

CHAPTER FOURTEEN
TROY

THE LAMBERT HOUSEHOLD WAS a mess when I pulled up. Jericho's Lexus blocked the whole driveway. The front door hung open, muffled sobs drifting out into the front yard.

I'm coming girls. It was the only thing on my mind as I surveyed the state of affairs and adjusted my plan. Inside the two-story house, I found Mr. and Mrs. Lambert crouched over Maddie. She was out cold, her silky brown hair matted to a bleeding gash on the side of her head.

My gut turned into a lead knot. They'd stay with her for now. I needed to secure Grace. I touched Mrs. Lambert's shoulder gently. She looked up at me with red-rimmed eyes.

I still hadn't met her parents face-to-face, but this wasn't the ideal time for introductions. I pressed a finger to my lips and then pointed up the staircase. She nodded, and I started a slow, silent creep up the stairs. As I ascended, I could hear the forced gentleness of a male voice.

"Come on Grace. It's me. It's time to go."

Jericho. At the landing, I peered around the corner. He stood at the end of the hallway, in front of an open bedroom door.

"It's me. Daddy. We're going now." He sounded agitated. Grace's whimpers leaked out of the bedroom.

"Why are you acting like this?" Jericho stomped into the room and I took my chance to slip down the hallway. I listened in for a second, calculating the best plan given his potential reaction. I didn't want Grace to see anything scary, even though I knew Jericho's entire presence was terrifying enough right now. I needed to subdue Jericho and drag his ass out of this house, without Grace seeing any of it.

A tall order, given the layout of this house. But I'd figure out a way.

"We need to go. Now. Where is your coat?" Jericho snapped.

"I want Mommy," Grace whimpered.

"She's not coming. You're coming with Daddy. What is so fucking hard to understand about that?" Jericho let out a frustrated sigh. "Listen, do you want any of these toys or whatever? Pick out something, let's go."

"Where's Mommy?" Grace was sobbing now. I couldn't stand another second of it. I stepped into the doorway, pinning Jericho with my gaze. He blanched when he spotted me.

"Toy!" Grace's bottom lip trembled and she moved toward me, but Jericho yanked at her arm.

"You're not going with him. He's bad. A bad man. You're coming with Daddy."

Grace's shoulders shook as she cried.

"Gracie-bell," I started, my voice calm. "You should listen to your daddy." I only said it because if I didn't, he'd become violent. Every inch of my skin prickled with awareness, with readiness. It was a type of trigger finger snap judgment that only came out under duress.

"See? Smart man. Bad, but smart." Jericho sneered at me. When he bent down to scoop up Grace, she wriggled away from him, screeching.

"No!"

"Grace. We're leaving." He lunged for her again and she darted away, an ear-piercing wail slicing through the air.

"Shut the fuck up," Jericho snarled.

"Let her pick where she wants to go," I blurted, my eyes on Grace's pained expression. My heart was splitting in two. I didn't understand how Jericho could willingly inflict this on his own flesh and blood. "Look at her. She's scared. If she wants to go with you, she will. But you need to let her choose."

Jericho huffed as though this was the stupidest idea he'd ever heard. "I'm her father. It doesn't matter what she wants. It matters what *I* want."

"Okay. But you have to understand that she's going to make your life hell if you take her out of here scared like this," I told him. "Let her choose. It'll be smoother." I stepped into the room, placing myself at Jericho's side. I had my palms lifted, to show him that I wasn't a threat, and that I was all-in on Grace making this decision. "This will be easier for her."

Jericho rolled his eyes. Then he cleared his throat, as though preparing to recite lines. "Grace. Who do you want to leave with? Me, or the bad man?"

Grace couldn't even talk from how hard she cried.

But she pointed her little finger at me.

"You're safe, Gracie-bell," I said softly. "It's okay."

She edged closer to me.

"You're not leaving with him," Jericho snapped.

"Come here, sweetie," I encouraged her.

Grace sank to the floor, an immobile mess. Beyond the utter heartbreak of seeing her faced with this scary situation, all I could see were the next moves to get her to safety. Away from 'daddy'. So then I could deal with daddy myself.

"She didn't choose you," Jericho informed me. He took a step toward Grace, but I jutted my elbow into his side forcefully. A *whoomp* escaped him and he staggered to the side. I scooped up

Grace, holding her shaking body to mine as I raced out of the room. I pulled open a different bedroom door and dropped her inside.

"Stay here, I'll be right back," I promised her before pulling the door shut. It wasn't ideal, but it would protect her from what came next. That was the priority right now: minimize damages. Minimize trauma. Obliterate Jericho.

After what he'd done today, I considered this my blank check. And I fully intended to write the amount of my dreams in the blank space.

Jericho barreled into the hallway just after I shut the door. He charged at me, swinging his fist. I ducked, catching him at the chest and hauling him against the opposite wall. Drywall cracked behind him and I slid my hands to his neck, pinning him there.

"You need to knock it the fuck off," I hissed, pressing my thumbs into the hollow of his neck. I had no time to waste. He'd done enough damage, and I wasn't interested in proving my strength or battling it out. I wanted him subdued and carried out of here on a stretcher.

But Jericho wasn't so willing. He had more fight in him. Or maybe I underestimated him. He landed a punch into the side of my head that made me loosen my grip. He jerked away, headed for the room where Grace was hidden. He landed a hand on the doorknob. From inside, Grace's wails drifted out.

He's not getting in there. It was the only thought on my mind as I grabbed for his wrist, yanking him away.

"Stay away from her," I growled.

"She's my fucking daughter. Not yours. And I'll make sure you don't ever go near her again," Jericho spat. But his words lacked bite. These were empty threats and I could tell.

"You're the one who's about to be kept from your family. From behind bars." I hauled him up against the wall again, and then I landed a punch to his face that made him shut up. Blood trickled from his nose immediately.

"That was for what you did to Maddie down there." I punched him again, feeling the crack of bone beneath my fist. "And that's for scaring Grace." He was fading out of consciousness already, but I wasn't done. I punched him again. "And that's for the baseball bat to the knee, you asshole."

Jericho crumpled to the ground and I spat on him. My chest heaved as I struggled to catch my breath and assess whether or not he was really out. I half expected him to lunge at me, zombie style. But he remained slumped and unconscious. I dragged him by the arm pits to the top of the stairs. At the base, Maddie's parents were still gathered around her. Maddie's mother was openly crying.

"Jericho's out," I reported.

"We called the police," Maddie's dad said, touching his busted nose gently. "And the EMS. They're both on their way."

"Are you both okay?" I called down.

"We're fine," Maddie's mother said, her voice choked with tears. "Maddie's breathing but she's passed out."

"I'm going to secure Jericho before I bring Grace out," I told them. "I don't want her to see this."

I pulled him down the hallway, then kicked him into the open door of the spare room where Grace's toys were. Out of sight enough for now. But there was still one issue: what if he woke up? I looked around, trying to find a makeshift ziptie. The only thing that made sense to me was some sort of fabric. I tore the sleeve of his button-up clean off at the shoulder seam, then used his own shirt to bind his wrists behind his back. Done. I hurried back to the first bedroom, finding Grace huddled against the bed, her cheeks tear-stained.

"Gracie bell. It's me." I held out my hands, hoping I hadn't scared her away. "It's okay now. Everything's okay."

"Toy." Her bottom lip trembled. "I want my mommy."

"I know you do, sweetheart. Let's go see her, okay?"

She nodded hesitantly and I scooped her up, holding her close. Out in the hallway, I spotted the blood smears across the wall, the dents. I owed the Lamberts an apology. Fucking a guy up was never a clean job.

When we got to the bottom of the stairs, Maddie was awake and mumbling. Grace reached for her grandma, so I passed her to Mrs. Lambert, who rocked her while she cried into Grace's hair. Maddie's father squeezed my shoulder.

"Thanks, son." Emotion shone in his eyes, and I didn't have the words to tell him how easily I'd do it all again if I had to.

"You're welcome, sir. I hope he doesn't give you guys any trouble anymore. I'm going to go check on him while we wait for the police." Before I did that, I bent down to look at Maddie. She had a nasty gash on the side of her head, but she was as beautiful as ever. I took her chin gently between my thumb and forefinger.

"Maddie. Can you see me?" I wasn't sure what type of damage that prick had done. I only knew he'd never be laying a finger on her again.

She mumbled something then nodded.

"You're safe. We're gonna get you to a hospital now, okay?"

She sighed, her eyes fluttering open. "Thank you, Troy."

"No need to thank me." I squeezed her chin gently, glad that I could get lost in the pretty depths of those hazel eyes once more. Men like Jericho could easily have taken it too far. "I did what needed to be done for my girls."

The small smile that curled her lips was one I wanted to never forget.

It didn't matter where I went next or how long I was gone.

She and Grace were mine.

CHAPTER FIFTEEN
MADDIE

My visit to the hospital resulted in three lovely new stitches, a very scared daughter who clung to my side endlessly...and a big, bear-like bodyguard who wouldn't leave my side either.

I spoke with the police while the nurses got my prescriptions, putting through my report for the incident with the tire slashing and what happened this morning. Everything was made much easier thanks to Troy's expert suggestion to use my cell phone as a recording device—tucked in my back pocket. The outrageous things on the recording were forwarded to the police, and would be used in the custodial dispute moving forward. Troy stood by my side, my hand in his big paw, while Grace curled up in my lap. My mom and dad flitted in and out of the room, offering details when necessary.

After I'd given up all the information they needed to begin the protection order, I looked up at Troy.

"Thank you for being here with me," I whispered.

"Leaving was never an option." His jaw flexed, and I could tell he was holding himself back from kissing me. We hadn't exactly told my parents what was going on. Hell, I don't think even we fully knew what was going on. But now that we were holding hands in front of them, they'd surely have questions for me later.

I looked at his thick fingers wrapped around my hand. "But your flight leaves tomorrow."

"I already called Nash and told him I'm missing it."

Tears welled up in my eyes. "Troy. You can't do that."

"Well, I did."

"You'll lose the job."

"I might. But I'll figure it out later. I don't want you to worry about it though." He leaned down, glancing at my parents before pressing a kiss to my lips. "I want to be here right now, so I'm here."

I couldn't argue with that. I worried he was missing out on a huge opportunity, but I couldn't change his mind.

Once I got the green light to leave, we returned to my parents' house. The house looked and felt strange after what happened in there with Jericho. My mother ushered me and Grace into the great room to relax, while she and my father and Troy worked on cleaning up the house. Based on how long I'd been knocked out, the doctor told me to take it easy—and that meant I'd get some time off of work. My head felt fuzzy, but I was otherwise fine. If a baseline level of distress and anxiety was considered fine.

But Troy made it melt away. Just one look at his handsome smile and his broad shoulders made everything better. He waited on me hand and foot, and even surprised Grace with a few rounds of Twisty Monkey to cheer her up. My baby girl was despondent and skittish after what had happened. It broke my heart to see her grappling with making sense of it all.

When dinner rolled around, my mom made a big deal about making sure Troy stayed to eat. I was certain, at this point, that he would have waited outside the front door like a puppy if he hadn't been invited. But my parents were hardcore Troy fans after what happened this morning, so there was no chance in hell my mother wouldn't insist on feeding this man forevermore.

"Is there anything I can do to help?" His rough baritone made my thighs clench, even when convalescing.

"Oh, you are too sweet. Just take this bread basket over for me." My mom handed him a wire basket stuffed with warm rolls. He helped carry things from the kitchen to the dining room table—my mom loved the fact that a man offered to do anything in the kitchen, since even my own father tended to be gone when it came time to set the table. Once everything was set, my mom called out for me.

"Dinner's ready! Oh, shoot—do you need help, honey?"

"I got it." I slowly pushed myself to sitting in the recliner where I'd been lounging all evening. Troy was at my side in a flash.

"I've got you." He offered his arm, which I took gratefully.

"You keep this up, my mom is liable to adopt you," I warned him. "You saved my life. Helped her in the kitchen. Now you're being my personal walker."

"Whatever it takes to get on the Lamberts' good side," he said.

"Oh, you're on their good side. Trust me. If they had to kick one of us out from dinner, I'm pretty sure they'd pick me."

Troy laughed richly as we shuffled toward the dining room table. I felt okay when I was sitting, but being upright and mobile made me woozy. Once we were all settled around the dining room table and tucking into mac and cheese and pork loin, my mom finally asked the question.

"So tell me, you two." She waved a knife between us, narrowing her eyes as though she'd guessed the secret. "Have you made it official?"

Troy and I shared a warm look. There was still so much more we needed to talk about. But how could I even hope to stop thinking about this man?

"It's up to your daughter," Troy said with a big smile to my parents.

"We haven't really talked about it," I said slowly, fighting a grin as I cut into my pork loin.

"I'm sorry! I'm zipping my lips!" My mom mimicked zipping her lips shut and throwing away the key. "But I do have one more question. Troy, do you need a place to stay? We have extra room for you if you need it."

He looked at me first for permission. When I nodded—entirely unable to contain my cheek splitting grin anymore—he said, "I'll take you up on that. I'm supposed to be heading back to New York soon but I'm not sure what my plans are anymore. Also, I owe you and Mr. Lambert some new drywall after what happened upstairs this morning."

"You don't owe us anything," my father insisted. "We owe *you*."

Dinner was lighthearted and yummy, and for a moment, things felt normal. Like we hadn't lived through a home invasion and assault only half a day earlier. I was ready for bed earlier than normal though, my headache driving me upstairs. My mom got the spare room ready for Troy while Grace and I showered and got into pajamas. There was no way Grace was going anywhere but at my side tonight, and I worried the whole ordeal had traumatized her. Troy came in to say goodnight to us, showering me with all the pent-up kisses from throughout the day.

"Thank you for being incredible," I whispered through the kisses.

"Mommy's face has a boo boo," Grace asserted. Troy and I paused, looking at each other before laughing.

"It definitely has a boo boo," I told her.

Troy squeezed my hand, kissing the back of it. "I've got a call with the Nightingales first thing in the morning."

The mention of his trip had a sobering effect. "Let me know what happens."

"You're the first to know," he promised me. "Do you need anything before you two go to sleep?"

I drew a deep breath, snuggling back into my bed. Despite everything that had happened today...I was at peace.

The only thing I needed to figure out was what happened when Troy eventually left?

I wanted to believe that we could maintain this connection no matter how far he traveled or how long he was gone. But the truth was...I had no idea.

And right now, my brain was too fuzzy to think about it.

The last thing I saw before I drifted off was Troy's handsome face.

CHAPTER SIXTEEN
TROY

Nash Nightingale called at nine a.m. on the dot.

He wasn't happy that I wasn't getting on the private jet with him.

"Louisville, huh?" He expelled a sigh.

"I need to be here for at least another day." I'd explained to him the *why*. It helped that I framed Maddie as a client needing additional protection. "But I'm hopeful you'll still consider me even though I missed the mark today."

Nash was quiet for a few moments. Then he said, "What if we picked you up?"

"Sorry?"

"We can swing through Louisville and get you on our way south."

"That would mean postponing the trip," I said slowly.

"I've got some flexibility," Nash said smoothly. "Do you?"

"I sure do."

"Great. Let's plan on that, then. We'll see you in two days."

I hung up the phone, both relieved and feeling sick. This meant I was actually leaving Maddie and Grace behind. I knew Maddie would understand. But dread coated my insides as I imagined this next chapter. Because deep down, I didn't believe it could work.

How could it? Maddie and Grace in Louisville, and me, everywhere but. Maybe it could work if they traveled alongside me, but that was impossible. Maybe it could work if I got a desk job in Louisville, but that was impossible too.

The only thing that was certain was that I had no idea what it might look like moving forward. And that's what I told Maddie when I shared Nash's new plan after my call.

"I want to be with you, Maddie," I told her. "I want you and Grace in my life. But I don't know how it's gonna look. I've never done this shit before and honestly, I'm out of my element."

She nodded, rubbing her thumbs over my knuckles. She sat cross-legged on the bed in front of me, wearing only an oversized t-shirt as pajamas. I'd never seen her look so delicious, but now was not the time to feast.

"I want to be with you too," she said softly.

"I'll travel a lot. But I want to know that my sexy schoolteacher is here waiting for me for when I get back." That earned me a smile. "So let's try this. Whatever it looks like." I brought the back of her hand to my lips, getting lost in her hazel eyes. "It can be something new. Something just for us."

"Just for us," she repeated, and then leaned forward to capture my lips in a kiss.

Quito. Cusco. Medellin. Panama City.

I accompanied Nash Nightingale's crew across all of South America for weeks on end. And every morning and night, I started and ended my day with Maddie and Grace.

Without fail.

Some nights, we'd be on the video call while Grace colored and Maddie cleaned up the kitchen or worked on school paperwork. Other nights, Maddie and I were lying in bed together, chatting about the future. And sometimes, when Grace was asleep and I knew I wouldn't be overheard by my travelmates, Maddie and I had *adult fun.*

We'd fallen asleep together on the video call. We'd watched movies while on video call.

It was fucking wild. Like living a dream that felt too good to be true. Here I was, traveling the world *and* dating a woman. I could be on the move, *and* let someone else into my heart. I hadn't realized the two could co-exist.

For now, it was enough.

Nash Nightingale was a good employer. He was rough around the edges, got a little too drunk and prone to annoying songs sometimes, and could talk circles around anyone who dared utter a word about real estate. When he had beer, he could speak Spanish, and when he had whiskey, he could speak French. For a poor kid from an old steel town in Ohio, he'd come a long way. That's what I related to the most. He didn't have a stable father figure growing up—never even knew who his father was to begin with—and spent his life trying to claw his way out of poverty. Just like the rest of us in the Fairchild orbit.

He and I hit it off fast. It was evident by the end of week one that we were a good fit. By the end of week two, we'd gotten drunk together. By week three, Maddie had lured Nash onto a video call one night and roped him into the accountability plan for me taking care of my knee. And by the end of week four, we were finally considering coming back to the US. Nash and his twin brother Archer were somewhere between boss and brother for me. So when they began laying out plans for the upcoming year, I knew that New York was my new base.

It had to be. That's where they needed me, and that's what made sense.

Which meant my tenure in Seven's apartment, looking after Jordan's weird-ass cat Ranger, was back in the forecast.

It just didn't leave a lot of time for visits to Louisville. That was the part I was trying to figure out. We could be long distance for a time. But I wanted her in my arms every night. That was the goal.

After Nash's South American "test trip", I finagled a stopover in Louisville. I got four days before they needed me back in New York, when I'd drive north from Louisville in my Jeep. Four magical days with Maddie and Grace...I *hoped*.

When I pulled up to her parents' house in early March, I felt like I was in a dream. My muscles were coiled tight with anticipation of seeing them again. Seeing if these daily video calls for the past month had really passed as a relationship.

Maybe I was deluding myself.

Maybe the bottom would fall out on this any second.

Grace was the first to burst out of the door. She was dressed in a winter coat and boots, clearly dressed and waiting for me to arrive. I picked up the cute little blondie and spun her around as she shrieked with excitement. "Toy!"

Well if that wasn't fucking worth the four week absence, I didn't know what was.

But then came Maddie.

She burst out of the house next, racing my way with the biggest, prettiest grin on her face. My heart nearly stopped beating as I drank her in. Brown wisps of hair escaped her topknot as she shrieked and launched herself into my arms. I received her jump-hug easily, my heart racing a mile a minute.

"God, we missed you!" She cinched her arms around my neck, laughing wildly as I hoisted her.

"I missed you more." I couldn't wait any longer. I kissed her, my tongue finding hers instantly, onlookers be damned. Her thighs squeezed around my torso as my hands slid to cover her ass. A groan began to rumble out of me, until Grace's little voice broke through.

"Mommy has a boo boo again," Grace said.

We dissolved with laughter. I squeezed the melons of her ass cheeks, pulling back enough to kiss the tip of her nose.

"Hello. I'm ten seconds away from defiling you in your parents' driveway."

She giggled, pressing her forehead to mine. "Is that a promise?"

"Or a threat. Not sure which. Fuck, I missed you."

"We should go inside. My parents are obsessed with you and need to tell you how much they love you." Maddie wriggled against me and I loosened my grip, letting her slide to the ground. "How much time off did you get?"

I bit my bottom lip as I sized her up. Juicier than fucking ever. I found her hand and brought it to my lips. "Four days."

I caught the slightest beginning of disappointment crashing across her face, but she perked up quickly. "We'll make the best of it. Let's go in."

"Hey. Guess what?"

A knowing grin curled at her lips. "You went to the doctor."

"I did. In Quito. Radiology and all."

"Well?" She watched me expectantly.

"My meniscus was fucked up. You were right."

She gasped and swatted at my chest while Grace hopped excitedly around us. "See? Don't doubt me."

"It was never doubt, baby. Just distraction. You think I'd give up precious seconds with you to go spend it with some ugly dude in a white coat?"

Grace jumped in front of me, wriggling her fingers so I'd pick her up. I scooped her up into my arms and found Maddie beaming at me.

"I'm glad you swallowed your pride and finally went." She squeezed my bicep. "And now you can heal it, but this means you're not carrying me anymore. You better listen to your schoolteacher from here on out."

Fuck. I loved it when she talked like this. "Yes, Miss Maddie." I couldn't resist—I dipped down for a kiss. Before I pulled away, I whispered so only she could hear, "But if you won't let me carry you, this just means that you need to sit on my face instead."

Her cheeks flushed and she bit at her bottom lip.

Grace squirmed in my arms, giggling. "Mommy and Toy kiss."

I followed Maddie inside, my gaze coasting over her curves. Now that I was mere feet away from her, it was hard work to keep myself off her. Her parents were just inside the door, which meant they'd probably seen me tonguefuck their daughter. *Oops.*

"Troy! It's so good to see you again!" Mrs. Lambert hugged me tightly. When she released me, Mr. Lambert had a hand waiting for me.

"How was South America, son?" The sincerity in his question paired with the sparkle of admiration in his eye did something to the little boy inside me who'd always fantasized about having a stable dad. I didn't begrudge my father for his mental illness—I'd long accepted him for who he was—but there was something that sparked in that moment. Grace danced in my arms, pumping her fists for "Toy!"

I'd never had the stable dad like Maddie did. And now Grace didn't either. But maybe I could be something like that role model to this sweet little blondie in my arms.

Even though I had no role model, she was already looking at me with those hearts in her eyes. Jericho hadn't respected that, or cherished it, but I would.

"South America was awesome. But it's been a long month," I told the family as Maddie shed her coat and boots and then helped Grace lose the layers. "I'm glad to be back."

"We hope you'll stay here while you're in town." Maddie's mom patted my arm. "Our house is yours. Always."

"There's no place I'd rather be." I brought Maddie's hand to my lips for a kiss. Because I fucking meant it.

We just needed to figure out a way that we could have more time together than four days every month.

And I had an idea.

CHAPTER SEVENTEEN
MADDIE

TROY TOOK ME OUT to a downtown Louisville restaurant for a "one month-iversary", as he called it, even though the date had passed while he was down south.

The man had come back tanned and more toned than when he'd left, and to this mid-winter white girl, he looked like a deity. He practically had a halo of sexiness around him, and I had to force myself to stop drooling whenever I looked at him for too long.

This didn't seem like real life. He was too hot. Too good. There had to be a flaw, and I already knew what it was: *too transient.*

It was the fear lapping at the edges of my thoughts. I was already thinking ahead, living in the future, trying to figure out what it might feel like after a year of doing the long-distance thing. Would we even be able to keep it up that long? Sure, we'd gotten into a nice groove while he was in South America. But now that routine was changing, and my entire existence hinged on routines. I gulped down the martini that the server had dropped off, eager to drown out my anxieties.

Troy lifted a brow. "Thirsty?"

"Parched." I sent him a shy smile, and he had the gall to look absolutely enamored. I could have come bare-faced and in my pajamas for this date night and he would probably still look at me like this. My heart pounded in my chest. After so long away from him, battling these intense feelings, I wasn't sure how to launch this conversation. Partly because I didn't know what I wanted to say other than *I love you.*

And that seemed out of the question.

"Everything okay?" Troy asked it offhandedly as he perused the menu board. This was the type of place to only have a small handful of entrees, printed on parchment and fastened to a piece of upcycled wood. Everything was low lit and wood fired in here. It was absolutely enchanting. I wanted to crawl into Troy's lap and never leave.

"Yeah. I'm just..." A million potential responses leapt to mind, but none made the leap to my tongue. "I'm trying to figure out what makes sense."

"Are you thinking of the wagyu?" He set down the menu.

"No, I mean—" I laughed at the misinterpretation. "In my *life.*"

"Oh. Well there's still a place for wagyu, either way," he teased. "But talk to me. What is it?"

I drew a deep breath. "When will I see you next?"

His face fell. "I don't know."

I nodded, looking down at the menu board without really seeing the text. "That's what I figured."

"It won't be terribly long," he hurried to add. "I've been thinking about spending weekends here. Or whatever days end up being the off days in my schedule. Maybe two days per week here, if I can time the flights right..."

I nibbled at my lip as he spoke, trying to imagine the future he laid out. It would be so much travel for him. But maybe....

"And then I wanted you and Grace to come up north and be with me in the city as soon as you could visit." He fiddled with his knife as he spoke. "The custodial stuff will be settled soon. You get summer breaks. That could be in New York."

I nodded. I'd been granted an uncontested divorce since Jericho's life was in shambles now. There was no chance he'd get partial custody, even if he got his act together soon, thanks to what we captured in those recordings from the assault. For the first time in my life, I felt free. Finally. "But what about after that?"

A heartbreaking grin graced his lips. "You're thinking that far ahead about us?"

I felt my cheeks redden. The server came up to take our orders, but without a moment's hesitation, Troy shook his head, lifting a finger. "Give us five." The waiter disappeared wordlessly and I leaned forward.

"Troy. I was ready to order."

He leaned forward too. "I need to hear what you have to say. Ordering can wait. But I'll call him back if you want me to."

I laughed, swatting his arm. "Why is it so hot when you prioritize?"

"I know what turns schoolteachers on."

I covered my mouth to hide the laugh. Troy looked immensely pleased with himself.

"All right. So yes, I'm thinking that far ahead about us. I just...I need to know how this is going to work." My real fears began tumbling out. "I loved the video chatting. We made it work. It was seamless. But I...I need something more concrete than that. Your schedule has the potential to change every month. I guess all of this has come up because..."

Troy narrowed his eyes. "Because what?"

"I've been looking at condos in Louisville." I nibbled on my bottom lip, hesitantly meeting his gaze. "I think it's time to leave my parents' house. I'm ready for my own space, I've got the down payment ready. We've been there for so long. But...I don't know..."

"What are you asking, Maddie?" His voice came out a sexy rasp.

"I don't know," I hissed, "isn't that obvious?" I covered my face with my hands.

Troy reached for my hand, which I gave him. He brushed his thumb back and forth across my knuckles. "I've been a nomad my whole life. I knew there would be a transition involved in getting serious with you..."

I swallowed hard, nodding.

"But there's one thing I'm certain of, and it's that I can't go on without you two in my life." His brown eyes were so soulful, I could hardly find my breath. "I need my girls. That's a non-negotiable. I know we'll find a way."

Tears pressed at my eyes. And our server was coming back again. When he showed up with a hopeful smile, Troy sent him away.

"They need Do Not Disturb signs for the tables," Troy muttered. My shoulders shook with laughter. I sniffed hard, dabbing at my eyes.

"I know you think we'll find a way," I said slowly. "But what *is* that way?"

Troy's intense gaze nearly crippled me. He didn't have the answer any more than I did. I only had a half-formed wish that I was too scared to follow.

"There's something you're not saying," he said.

"I want to go to New York with you," I blurted. My cheeks immediately heated up. I was aware how it sounded. "To visit. I mean—spring break is starting next week..."

His brows shot up. "Done. Let's go, babe."

I laughed into my palm. "I didn't want to force myself onto your plans..."

"You're not forcing anything. I want this too. And when you come visit, then we can see how you feel about staying longer than just spring break." He winked at me before pressing a kiss to my knuckles, then he finally leaned back and flagged the server. "Now it's time to order."

Two days later, I found myself in the middle of Tribeca.

In Seven's apartment. AKA Troy's current home.

Looking around at the exposed brick and the stripper pole and the leather couches feeling like I was back at that Christmas party from three months ago.

Life had certainly changed since then, and only for the better. Three months ago, I was terrified of Jericho. Wondering if I'd ever find my way. Now, I was enjoying life in a way I never imagined possible. Even amid the routine and the responsibilities, I felt a freedom I'd never had before.

Maybe it had always been there, even if it had been restricted by my relationship with Jericho. But Troy certainly helped me tap into it.

Troy wrapped an arm around me, pressing his lips to my temple. Grace was in his arms, fiddling with his beard.

"How's it feel to be back?"

We'd just arrived to the city after breaking up the long car ride into two days with a stopover in Pennsylvania. I was brimming with excitement. Everything about New York City felt alive and fresh. Not to mention my best friend and former sister-in-law, Mercedes, was here. Our plan was to simply settle in this first evening. I hadn't even texted Mercedes yet.

"So amazing." I let out an incredulous laugh and flitted to the big windows overlooking the street. I stared down at the cars and the activity below. My heart thudded in my chest as I imagined all the things I'd like to do during the trip. "I don't even know where to begin with my to-do list. We only have a week here?"

"Unless you decide to make it longer." Troy winked at me. Ranger meowed, annoyed, from the far edge of the apartment. We'd already fed him, but he still seemed to regard me and Grace with suspicion. "Ranger, what's your deal?"

"I think he doesn't like us being here," I teased. I used the tried and true *ps-ps-ps* and held out my fingers but Ranger didn't budge. He actually seemed to glare at me as he prowled closer to Troy. I didn't even know cats could glare. "I think he's jealous."

"Ranger, stop. You know you're my number one street cat." Troy wandered toward the stripper pole and Ranger followed. "You're gonna have to get used to Maddie being here, ya old man. She'll be staying after spring break, won't she?"

"If I could commute. Though the commute would kill me," I murmured as I dragged my finger along the wooden frame of the window. "Not to mention a physical impossibility."

"That's why you ditch the commute and just stay." Troy and Grace had migrated over to the pole, where they'd made a game out of her grabbing for the pole and him pulling her away just before she caught it. She was shrieking with laughter after several failed latch attempts.

"What's this game called?" I asked over the laughter.

"Twisty Stripper," Troy joked.

"Twisty Tipper!" Grace echoed.

He and I shared a stunned look, then we both burst out into laughter. "I'll be sure to tell Jordan about the new game named in her honor." I sank into the couch, expelling a happy sigh. We had just under a week ahead of us. I looked forward to exploring the city with Grace and spending time with Mercedes and her family while Troy worked. And then...back to real life.

That was the part I wasn't looking forward to.

I wanted real life to feel like the thing I looked forward to. My entire marriage to Jericho had felt like one long dread spiral. I always dreaded him coming home. Dreaded our vacations. Dreaded making him upset.

That wouldn't be the case with Troy. But we needed a day-to-day to look forward to. Not just the fringes of our separate existences.

A knock on the front door interrupted my thoughts. I twisted to look at the door, then over at Troy, who had Grace mid-air on her way to the pole.

"Are you expecting anyone?" I asked before hopping to my feet.

"No, but knowing the Fairchild crew, it could be any one of them behind that door. Or all of them."

I laughed, checking my phone on my way. Nothing from Mercedes. As I neared the door, I heard the undertones of voices. Maybe it was Mercedes and Trace. But those booming undertones didn't sound like her...I peered through the peephole, seeing the backs of a few broad-shouldered men. I frowned, looking back at Troy, who picked up on my concern.

"I'm coming." He carried Grace in his arms in the plane position. She shrieked with laughter, holding out her arms as she zoomed along with him. He peered through the peephole first too, then pulled open the door. "Well my god..."

The amusement in his voice calmed me. The door swung open, revealing some familiar faces. Trace, with Willow in his arms, and Seven stood before us; Mercedes poked her head out from behind Trace next. Next to Seven there was an unfamiliar face, but his icy blue eyes reminded me of someone I'd seen a time or two on video chats.

"Oh my God!" I squeaked.

"You're *heeeere*!" Mercedes surged forward and pulled me into a hug, laughing wildly. Her baby bump was so much bigger than the last time I'd seen her, and I could feel it pressing into my belly. Boisterous greetings were exchanged between all of us, Grace immediately squealing with excitement that her bestie Willow was here. After we exchanged hugs and I formally shook Nash Nightingale's hand, the eight of us moved deeper into the apartment. Warmth flooded the room, filling me from head to toe with contentment.

"This is such a surprise!" I watched as Seven unloaded some big bags onto the island.

"You have Trojan to thank for that," Seven said with a shy smile. He looked over at his best friend. "He sent me on a wild goose chase for this specific cheese board."

Tears pricked at my eyes as I looked over at Troy. He watched me with so much love in his eyes that it was hard to look away, or even remember that there were other people in the room.

"Gotta get weird cheese for my girl," Troy said simply. "And there's no weirder cheese than in NYC."

"Yeah, it's kinda the sort of thing you might want to have more regularly," Mercedes said brightly, popping in a cube of cheese as Seven unwrapped the board. She got first dibs, as the one currently growing a human. But I was next in line. I picked a cube and popped it in my mouth. Something smoked and buttery melted in my mouth and I let out a happy hum.

Holy shit. This was what it felt like to have a community. A real, grounded network. Jericho had deprived me of that for so long. I barely had any friends back in Kentucky thanks to his efforts to distance me from my high school and college friends.

"God, this is good. Nash, please have some."

"I don't want to interrupt your fun family night guys," Nash said, his husky baritone the sort of voice that women paid money to hear. "I'm just here to drop off the keys." He revealed a set of keys, grinning over at Troy, who returned the look.

I narrowed my eyes. Troy was keeping something from me.

"What're the keys for?" I asked.

Nash looked at me guiltily. "I think that's for him to explain. But just know, this guy loves you a whole lot. And I'm happy to support my family man bodyguard."

"See, this is why I wanted to be here," Seven said, reaching for a cheese cube.

Mercedes rolled her lips inward, looking like she was trying to keep herself from bursting.

Nash squeezed Troy's shoulder and waved at the rest of us, heading for the door. "Enjoy your evening, friends." We all called out our goodbyes and when the door shut I looked around at everyone.

"Guys..." I started.

Troy set the keys on the kitchen island and then scooped my hands into his. "Maddie, it's no secret I'm fucking crazy about you. I want you and Grace in my life forever. I'm yours, and you two are mine. There's no question about that. So when Nash and I negotiated our contract, I made sure to include some provisions for...the future."

Emotion swelled in my chest. I almost couldn't believe my ears. "Yeah?"

"I've got a company car now that's better equipped for a family. My Jeep is going into storage. And these keys are for the condo I'm renting."

Mercedes made a little squeak, but I couldn't rip my eyes off Troy.

"I'm sorry," she whispered. "The hormones are making it impossible to keep my excitement in."

"What condo are you renting?"

"It's up to you...but I thought you'd be most comfortable living a bit closer to family." Troy's heartbreaker grin came out to play as he rubbed his thumb back and forth across my knuckles. Then he looked over at Mercedes. "Do you want to tell her?"

"Maddie, he rented the condo right beneath where we live!" Her words came out rushed and loud, and I could tell it was a major relief for her to finally get it out. I covered my mouth with a hand, the tears already blurring my vision. "It's above a *bookstore*," she added.

"Oh my God," was all I could muster.

"I know we're just starting out," he went on. "But I'm all in. And whenever you choose to come live here full-time, just know that I'm ready."

My ears rang from the warring pressures of excitement and disbelief. Was this real life?

"This is unbelievable," I said, and then the tears finally broke the dam and streamed down my cheeks. Troy scooped me up into his arms and I cried into his chest. The tenderness of his decisions—including me in his plans, leaving space for me to join, or not join, on my own terms—was somehow the hottest thing anyone had ever done for me.

When I looked up, I found tears in his eyes too. I pushed onto my tiptoes, pressing my lips to his in a long, sweet kiss.

"I love you, Troy." I cinched my arms around his neck and got lost in his warm, brown eyes. I never wanted to be anywhere else but here. In his arms.

"And I love you more, Maddie. I love you more than I even thought was possible."

He kissed me again, and the rest of our friends and family hooted and hollered.

I was ready to marry this man. Bear his children. Take his last name.

But first, I'd start with the weird cheese board and a spring break in New York.

We had the rest of our lives ahead of us.

EPILOGUE

TROY

"Monkey! Check out this slide!" I cupped my hand around my mouth to get Grace's attention from across the playground. We had made a slight detour on our walk around Tribeca that morning. It was my off day, and we made the best of our off days together. Not just because it was a gorgeous August summer day in New York City, but because life was about to get crazy.

School started next week, and Maddie was the newest 1st grade teacher at a private school just two blocks away from our condo. Her teaching certificate had been conditionally approved by the state of New York three weeks ago, and the moving van containing the last of her things had arrived only days after—driven by her parents, who'd been visiting for the past two weeks.

I caught Maddie's gaze from across the playground. She sat on a bench with her mom and dad, deep in conversation with them. The last I'd heard, they were considering getting a place up here as well, something that they could sublet as needed but also use as a base for when they visited. Her parents were also falling in love with the city, which was just perfect.

Because my monkey needed her grandparents too.

Shit was lining up so perfectly I could hardly believe it. I'd never made a more natural step than to bring Maddie and Grace into my life. Her transition into living full-time in New York happened as soon as the school year ended in Kentucky, which was also when she resigned from her job. And ever since the three of us had been happily sharing the Tribeca condo, I couldn't remember a time where we hadn't been living together.

It just felt right. It felt good. Even though part of me was still horrified I'd put down roots like this...I only wanted more.

My past didn't have to dictate my future. And here I was, having a fantastic fucking time as a family man. The thought made me grin as I lifted Grace onto the ledge of the slide.

"Toy! Let's go fast!"

I pushed her down the slide and she tossed her hands into the air, screeching with delight. Hell, I was having so much fun as a family man, I thought about making another little monkey with Maddie someday. But that would come once she got settled into the city and her new job. Now that I was six months into my job with Nash Nightingale, I was confident this job would extend...mostly because I'd signed onto a five-year contract with the brothers.

My phone rang just as Grace ejected from the bottom of the slide and ran around for another round. It was Nash. I answered the call, my gaze sliding back to Maddie. "Sup Nash?"

"Trojan. I'm not interrupting anything, am I?" His rough voice held an edge to it that I couldn't immediately place.

"No, no. Just went on a walk with Maddie and the fam. What's up?"

An uncharacteristic pause filled the air between us. Nash was a man who knew what he wanted to say and how to steer the conversation. So this hesitation felt like a warning.

"I might need to steal you for a few hours today," he finally said.

"Shit. Is everything okay?"

He expelled a sigh. "I got some major news and I...I'm honestly not sure what it all means yet. But Archer and I found out today that we are set to receive a pretty major inheritance...from a grandfather we never knew about."

My insides tightened. "Whoa. That's huge." Grace shrieked with glee as she zipped down the slide next to me. Thankfully, she'd figured out the slide-to-shriek pipeline on her own. "Wait, what grandpa?"

"Yeah, we had the same question." Nash laughed. "Someone from my biological father's family."

"The dad you never met or knew about?" I asked.

"Yeah. That one. Archer and I were listed as the recipients of this money and it stands to be a lot."

"How much?"

"Billions." He coughed. "But there's a catch."

"Do I want to know what it is?"

"According to the lawyer who reached out, Archer and I need to be legally married if we want to inherit the money."

I blinked a few times, digesting the weird stipulation. My gaze slid from Grace, who was making another round on the slide, over to Maddie and her parents, who were laughing at something together. "So you'll do it...right?"

His rich laughter filled my ear. "Hell yes. You know anyone who wants to be married long enough for me to inherit this cash?"

"The only unmarried lady I know is mine, and I don't share," I told him. As if on cue, Maddie looked my way and sent me a shy smile. I blew her a kiss, which she pretended to capture and press to her cheek. "I'm sure you can find someone..."

"Yeah. I'm working on it. Anyway, we don't want this to leak. Shit has been nuts lately anyway with the tabloids, so, if you could spare us an afternoon, I'd like you to come along for this meeting with the lawyer. I'm worried it could get weird. I don't even know who this family of ours is."

"I'm there." It wasn't a question. Nash had brought me into his family, and was financing the life of our dreams in New York. I knew Maddie would want me to be there too. And she'd hear all about it soon enough.

When Nash and I hung up, I assisted Grace on a few more rounds on the slide, until she got bored and we wandered toward the swings.

But not without a quick stop to kiss Mommy, from both me and Grace.

"I love you, Mommy," Grace said with a sweet smile. And then she swung her gaze up to me and grinned. "And I love you, too, Toy."

She skipped off toward the swings and I almost fucking cried.

I'd never get tired of hearing that.

I'd never get tired of being the man my girls needed.

I swooped down for my own kiss from Maddie, and then I followed behind Grace.

I was living the dream...the dream I never knew could actually be mine.

THE END

Get ready for Nash Nightingale and his marriage of convenience to single mom Clara in BOSSY BILLIONAIRE (http://books2read.com/bossy-billionaire).

If you haven't read about the Fairchilds in their books, you can catch up on their angsty & steamy romances in THE PRICE OF A PROMISE (book #1) (http://books2read.com/price-of -promise).

ACKNOWLEDGEMENTS

This book would not have been possible without the unending support of my husband & children – I made a surprise third book happen this year only because of this support!
Thank you to Elisabeth Nelson and Lainey Davis for help with the outline and the beta reading.
Endless thanks to my readers – without your voices, I might not have written this book! Your support and encouragement mean the world to me, and I love being on this wild writer ride with you all!

LET'S STAY CONNECTED!

Stay connected with me via my newsletter, where I share teasers, sales, and other exciting news.

Or join my reader group, EMBER'S BLOSSOMS, to hang out up-close and personal! Early looks at new covers, exclusive access to ARC sign-ups, and more.
FACEBOOK
INSTAGRAM
GOODREADS
BOOKBUB
TIKTOK

Website for general book info:
http://www.emberleighromance.com/
Store for all the discounts, bundles, and deals:
http://www.emberleighstore.com

And before you go...

Please consider leaving an honest review about this book! Even just a few words or a line mean so much to us authors.

ALSO BY EMBER LEIGH

THE NIGHTINGALES OF WALL STREET
Broken Bodyguard
Bossy Billionaire

THE BAD BOYS OF WALL STREET
The Price of Revenge
The Price of Passion
The Price of Infamy
The Price of Forever

WINTER HARBOR
(co-written with Whitley Cox)
The Bastard Heir
The Asshole Heir
The Rebel Heir
The Matchmaking Heirs

THE BREAKING SERIES
Breaking the Rules
Changing the Game

Breaking the Sinner
Breaking the Habit
Breaking the Fall

THE BAYSHORE SERIES (The Keegans)
A Perfect Match

THE BAYSHORE SERIES (Daly brothers)
Make Me Lose
Make Me Fall
Make Me Yours
Make Me Choose
Make Me Hot
Make Me Smile

www.ingramcontent.com/pod-product-compliance
Lightning Source LLC
Chambersburg PA
CBHW031540310726
48971CB00008B/2560